PENGUIN BOOKS

Quill

Neil Drinnan was born in 1964 in Melbourne, and was dubiously educated at various (now defunct) high schools and Camberwell Boys' Grammar. He has worked in publishing for many years, and also writes for a number of magazines. He is the author of *Glove Puppet* and *Pussy's Bow*.

For mothers, sons and lovers in a 'never the twain' world

Neal Drinnan

Quill

A Novel

For Matty B
with
love

PENGUIN BOOKS

Penguin Books Australia Ltd
487 Maroondah Highway, PO Box 257
Ringwood, Victoria, 3134, Australia
Penguin Books Ltd
Harmondsworth, Middlesex, England
Penguin Putnam Inc.
375 Hudson Street, New York, New York 10014, USA
Penguin Books Canada Limited
10 Alcorn Avenue, Toronto, Ontario, Canada M4V 3B2
Penguin Books (NZ) Ltd
Cnr Rosedale and Airborne Roads, Albany, Auckland, New Zealand
Penguin Books (South Africa) (Pty) Ltd
5 Watkins Street, Denver Ext 4, 2094, South Africa
Penguin Books India (P) Ltd
11, Community Centre, Panchsheel Park, New Delhi 110 017, India

First published by Penguin Books Australia Ltd 2000

10 9 8 7 6 5 4 3 2 1

Cover design by John Canty, Penguin Design Studio
Text design by Cathy Larsen, Penguin Design Studio
Typeset in 11/16 Weiss and 9.5/16 Optima by Midland Typesetters, Maryborough, Victoria
Printed in Australia by Australian Print Group, Maryborough, Victoria

National Library of Australia
Cataloguing-in-Publication data:

Drinnan, Neal.

Quill.

ISBN 0 14 029099 0.

I. Title.

A823.3

www.penguin.com.au

Contents

Je Louse 1

Gridiron 139

Acknowledgements

With thanks to Tim for his love and support.

Special thanks to Alison Cowan for her magical editorial touch and to Julie Gibbs for her ongoing enthusiasm.

Je Louse

I

Accursed from their birth they be
Who seek to find monogamy
Pursuing it from bed to bed –
I think they would be better dead.

REUBEN'S CHILDREN, Dorothy Parker

A clot of guilt pulsed through the valves of Blaise's heart when Woodrow poked his head out the door. Woodrow looked curiously at his lover, who sat on their newspaper-strewn balcony. It was that heavy time of year in Sydney. Everything weighed twice as much as normal and even though autumn was just around the corner, summer lingered on. On and on.

'Whatcha reading?' Woodrow's words were cool and light.

'Oh, *Spectrum*, the book reviews. Elliot's just put another book out, it's called *Je Louse*.'

'*J'ai* crabs would be more like it. I thought we'd been through the Elliot thing?'

'It's an interview, for God's sake. I'm hardly going to *not* read it.' Blaise folded into himself, his neat brown hair too short to shield his eyes. He didn't want this discussion but it was going to happen, and his body always lurched into positions of defence and confession way before his mind had charted its course. 'You're such a puppy dog,' Elliot always used to say.

In truth, Blaise hadn't begun to read the review. He was busy looking at the photograph of Elliot Bernard and his playwright boyfriend, Lex Constantine. They were sitting beneath a Keith Haring painting on a large cream sofa in their Long Island home. Elliot was playfully fighting off a slobbering bloodhound while Lex smiled wryly, pretending to read the *New Yorker*. The heading read:

PAST TENSE: FUTURE CONDITIONAL.

'I don't see why you go on living in the past, Blaise. It stirs things up every time he puts another book out. And they're not even any good – I thought we'd agreed.'

'Woodie, I lived with him for six and a half years. I'm bound to notice these things.'

Woodrow snatched the *Spectrum* from his lover's hands, looked at the photo of *them*, pulled a face and tossed it over the balcony. It floated like a half-remembered dream into the lush tropical garden below. Blaise felt too proud to go down three floors and fetch it.

'How long before we can stop living in the shadow of Elliot-bloody-Bernard? We read the last book and it was a waste of trees.'

'I liked some of it.'

'Elliot's mind is an environmental hazard. You were glad to get away from all his games and deceptions. He used to cheat on you constantly – you said so yourself.'

'And who was I seeing for the last six months of *my marriage*, hey? Who did I leave him for?'

'What else could he expect? He treated you like shit.'

'He did not treat me like shit – I've never said that. We had some great times.'

'Yeah – right, him dragging his tired old box around every sex club in town is OK *now*, is it? Him living off your money for six months while he wrote that crappy first book . . .'

'It was his bloody flat, I didn't have to pay rent or anything and he was lecturing part-time.'

'Let's not get into this, Blaise. You were a mess when we moved in together. These days all you do is defend him. Perhaps you should fucking well go back to him now you've decided the sun shines out of his behind.'

Woodie was satisfied. He knew – they both knew – there was no chance of this last scenario transpiring. It was a ruse. Elliot Bernard now inhabited a different stratosphere. The cruelty of the truth didn't need to be laboured; it just hung there like cling wrap on the humidity, mingling at a nasty frequency with static from a neighbour's radio.

Blaise didn't bother to mention that the reason he had been in a mess was precisely *because* he'd left Elliot

Bernard, formerly Bernard Elliot. He didn't explain that even though he'd known the relationship was doomed, he still mourned its passing. He could never explain to Woodrow how some of Elliot's wayward morals had taught him more about life and emotional survival than he was learning from the increasingly stuffy and dysfunctional monogamous dynamics of this three-and-a-half-year cohabitation.

'I just don't think you should read that book – end of story.' Woodrow stormed into the bathroom.

Blaise felt a flush of anger and self-loathing that things should have come this far: that the article he so wanted to read was down in the shrubbery, that the house and car were in both their names. Blaise had entrenched himself. He felt he'd spent years doing anything he could to keep Woodrow happy – to avoid his outbursts. But the more he did, the more he had to do. It was like a treadmill. Some people are just like that. Treadmills.

11

In Viva Livre there stood an impressive pile of *Je Louse*. Elliot's latest book was hardcover – thirty-five dollars. Thirty-five dollars Blaise wouldn't be EFTPOSing from the joint account because Woodie would go through the bank statements with a fine toothcomb.

Blaise lurked guiltily around the display – an adulterer in a brothel. He could still walk away and remain faithful. His stomach gurgled – a hot wave of bile boiled through it while shame brightened his cheeks. *Why should I feel guilty about buying a book, for Christ's sake?*

A chiselled male physique with wild green, digitally enhanced eyes posed lasciviously on the cover. The figure seemed in motion. In the foreground were two chalice-like goblets, one had been knocked over by the model's muscly forearm and rich, crimson wine trickled down the ridges of his flat stomach. Red wine, or was it blood?

Blaise picked up a copy and stared at the author's photo on the back. It was a different shot to the one in his last book. Elliot had been salvaged from the rigours of a decade by air-brushes and clever studio lighting. He looked more like a man in his late twenties than one in his late thirties, though there was that knowing in his eyes, that bleary decadence which somehow inspired trust and risk in the same moment. His hand was poised thoughtfully near his mouth and his tight white shirt was stretched across his chest. Blaise's heart fluttered; the author still wore the ring Blaise had given him on their fifth anniversary.

Woodrow would think it weird if he knew Elliot still wore a ring given to him by an ex-lover. Woodrow thought it was all or nothing with relationships, and he had no contact with his exes. It was as if he hated them all, as if they had ceased to exist and accidental meetings were invariably torturous affairs. With Woodrow it was as if pain, once granted, could never be rescinded, healed or forgiven. As though things weren't worth anything unless they were forever. *And how many things last that long?* he pondered.

Blaise knew for a fact that both happiness and sadness were only ever just passing through – the perennial game of two-up. How had Elliot put it in *Intra Venus*? 'God's guinea pigs: ephemerally potent with hormonal tricks, capricious alchemies and star-governed emotions. Uppsie-Downsie dolls – turned one way for happy, one way for sad. Flippsie, floppsie – up, down, DEAD.'

Elliot's chest looked more defined in this photo than he remembered it. Blaise hadn't seen him for eighteen months and even then it had been at Mardi Gras or one of the other big parties – the briefest how-do-you-do. But success seemed to revive people, it offered a hiatus to ageing. An amnesty against the worldly day-to-day grinding down endured by ordinary folk. He searched the picture for familiarities and pondered his old lover's fortunes. *He probably goes to the gym all the time over there – clippers his chest hairs too, bet he gets dermabrasion, fruit acid peels and God knows what all.* He shivered with the sudden recollection of how Elliot used to smell. His body and soul buzzed with desire for a nanosecond. He opened to the back flap:

Elliot Bernard was born in rural New South Wales, Australia, and studied Literature at the University of Sydney. He has written two previous novels – *Intra Venus, Corpus Delicti* – and a collection of essays on sexual subversion in Australian literature entitled *Careful He Might Queer You.* He now leads a bi-coastal life in the United States, lecturing at Princeton and UCLA. His hobbies include worrying, hurrying and cooking. He lives on Long Island with his partner and a large bloodhound called Glasnost.

Blaise looked at the posters again:

In praise of *Je Louse*:

A sharply focused and deliciously rendered tour de force ...

A bittersweet, unforgettable portrait of modern gay love ...

Beware of ex-lovers with quills ...

Ex-lovers with quills?

Blaise opened to the first page:

Whom we love best, to them we can say least.

Oscar Wilde, THE PICTURE OF DORIAN GRAY

Those who are faithful know only the trivial side of love; it is the faithless who know love's tragedies.

ibid.

Bloody typical.

And the next page ...

'What are you reading, honey?'

'A review of Humphrey Calston's new novel.'

'I thought after the fiasco at his launch we weren't going to read any more of his books.'

'That was your decision, Wolfgang, not mine.'

Blaise slammed the book shut, blushing from the tips of his toes to the summit of his pate. Wolfgang could only be Woodrow. He hesitated before going in search of the other name – his own pseudonym in what he immediately suspected was a roman à clef. He gasped when he found it: 'Pascal'. Blaise Pascal, the French mathematician and philosopher. It was obvious – his French teacher used to harp on and on about Blaise Pascal; she had even quoted him from time to time.

He handed over the cash at the counter to a surly-looking fat girl with punk eye make-up and several facial piercings.

'He's got AIDS.'

Blaise was deep in a miserable trance. He frowned at her distraction. 'What?'

'He's got AIDS.'

'Who?'

'Elliot Bernard. Well, not AIDS, but he's HIV-positive. It was in *Christopher Street*.'

The girl was smiling enigmatically, as if this was good in some ironic way. As if this fact offered grim, succinct closure to some ghastly rumination in her Gothic scheme of things. Did she expect him to be impressed by the fact that she read *Christopher Street*, or was this some nightmare he needed to wake from? Blaise felt like yanking her nose ring. 'Take a pig to market' was the expression Elliot had used in a bondage scene from *Corpus Delicti*. But as usual he wondered if it was he who was actually reading things the wrong way. Why did the world drift so?

It was a component of Blaise's dark, delirious, inexplicable self to interpret the malevolent murmurs of strangers, drunks and bag ladies as omens or prophecies.

Once he spent all day wondering what was hidden in a drunkard's pronouncement, 'Yer'll know it when ya see it, ya poncy little nance.' He'd looked for *it* all day, sure that some special wisdom must be inherent in the livery-glug-glug of an alcoholic's verbal fire. 'The profundity or banality of urine-scented paper-bag princes who no longer bothered to drop their trousers for number ones or number twos always caught him unawares.' Blaise tapped the side of his head. He was starting to think in Elliot's prose; he wouldn't tolerate that.

Blaise knew very well that Elliot was HIV-positive. Knew better than most people, but to the girl it was no more intriguing than a TV actress with breast implants or a popular athlete with a penis extension.

'I'm much more into contemporary stuff. Elliot Bernard is too camp and eighties. Luke Davies, Irvine Welsh and Poppy Z Brite do the drug thing heaps better – sex too, if you ask me, but I'm just a shop girl so what would I know?'

Blaise guessed with all her attitude she wouldn't even be that for long.

'I can do without the commentary, thanks. I pretty much know what I like to read.' He wanted to go mad at her about the HIV. It really wasn't her business to broadcast that to all and sundry, but as it was in *Christopher Street* it would seem odd making a fuss. The girl pulled a face as she scanned and bagged the offending item.

'When you're lecturing at UCLA and spending your summers in Martha's Vineyard and Nantucket, then maybe you can sneer at other people's work and success.' Had he really said that?

She grimaced. 'Viva Livre – and have a nice day.'

He felt hopelessly un-hip and old at thirty. Nantucket, fuck-it.

Blaise felt violated, soiled and dissatisfied from his point-of-purchase encounter. He headed back to his office and the waiting pile of affidavits, contracts and sundry legal pap. He could not bear to read the book but could not tolerate doing anything else.

'Oh, bugger it!' He opened the tome on his desk.

> . . . Pascal and Wolfgang arrived late and sticky to the launch. Humphrey spotted them through the crowd as they gathered in the sweaty cluster of literati and party desperates. Moisture hung heavy and close from a Sydney sky. It threatened to vacuum seal the guests like supermarket olives if it didn't storm soon. It moistened brows and vexed armpits among the Mardi Gras crowd. Humphrey smiled to see Wolfgang was there too. After all this time Pascal obviously couldn't be trusted out on his own. He continued his speech . . .
>
> 'The price of liberty is eternal vigilance and while most Sydneysiders have gleaned this knowledge from reading the inscription on the RSL building in Rose Bay, it is our

community's motto every bit as much as theirs. But let's not forget, it is profitability that peoples the publishers' lists and while our emerging culture may appear to be a novelty, an adventure and a Kinder Surprise, we are yet to prove ourselves the geese that have laid the golden egg. I'd like to thank Jennifer Fitzherbert and Carl Beauman at Impala Press for taking this risk and for looking to a future that will surely be better in this ghetto thanks to the visionary courage of people like themselves.'

Humphrey descended into the applauding fray of smiling well-wishers, determined to speak to Pascal. After all, he had dedicated the novel to him regardless of the sad parting that had since come between them. It wasn't easy to reach the other side of the room. People waved pens and copies of *Fast Trax* at him. He kept looking out the corner of his eye for Pascal, who chatted to all the old friends they had once shared. Wolfgang lurked like a dark cloud; he seemed to drain a glass of champagne each time Humphrey glanced towards them. Finally the moment arrived.

'Hey Pascal, after all this time I've finally done it. Hi Wolfgang, I'm glad you could come.' Pascal kissed him. 'And I'm very proud of you, Humphrey.'

The two exchanged a glance that excluded Wolfgang. It signified their own past trials and tribulations, another life . . .

Michael Goldstein was at the door to Blaise's office. 'Have

you finished checking the Li file? They're here to sign the contract of sale.'

Blaise slammed the book shut and dropped it to the floor. 'Mike, can you give me ten minutes?'

'Alright, but make it quick – OK?'

Blaise's heart was thumping ten to the dozen. He couldn't focus on anything. He had to know what Elliot said about the launch. He proofed the documents sloppily and gave them to a secretary to print up with the changes he'd made. He slunk off to the bathroom, where he could snatch an unquestioned fifteen-minute break.

> . . . and other victories. Hot nights and wild sex, passionate ecstasies that Wolfgang never shared nor instigated, meaningful if forgotten penetrations in the distant hotels of far-off countries to which Wolfie had never been. Brisk walks in the Scottish Highlands or slow walks through the Met and the Guggenheim – precious memories understood only by Humphrey and Pascal.
>
> Wolfgang didn't hold his liquor well and didn't like the exclusive triumph of his lover's embrace with this newly celebrated writer . . .

Uh oh. Blaise paused fearfully. He almost couldn't bear to continue.

> . . . Wolfgang swayed uncertainly, his mouth fighting to smile but his eyes smouldering like burning peat. 'So is *Fast Trax* the gourmet's guide to the sex venues of Sydney?'
>
> 'Not quite, Wolfgang. Mostly it's set in New York, but

there are plenty of sex clubs in the Meat Packing District which the book explores *unflinchingly*.'

'And I bet you know every one of 'em . . .' He hiccupped on the 'em. 'Bet you've done some meat packing of your own down there . . .'

'That's enough, Wolfie,' hissed Pascal through gritted teeth.

'It's alright, Humphrey knows me, don't you Humphrey? And I know him. We know each other.' He winked at the author, 'And, moreover, he's proud of his exploits in the sex clubs, aren't you Humphrey? I read that article in *Outrage* where you said love was meant to be spread around and you've always spread it around. HIV didn't even slow you down, did it, you old wolf? The virus was the sachet of lube that shot you into the true realms of depravity.'

'Stop it, Wolfgang, this is fucking embarrassing.'

Humphrey's smile remained pasted like a restroom fixture to his otherwise impassive face. He was looking for an escape; his publicist, agent, publisher – anyone important would do.

'He doesn't mind, do you Hump . . . Humphrey? I know Humphrey and he knows me. God wouldn't have given us two holes if he hadn't meant us to fill 'em, would he Humphrey?'

'I dare say not, Wolfgang. Look, can you both excuse me? I can see my agent, Natasha. She's looking rather lost – I must rescue her.'

Pascal wandered towards the door with his drunken lover. Humphrey's departure was the last humiliation for the night – an agent in Sydney looking lost at a book launch, who ever heard of such a thing?

'OK Wolfie, let's go. You've spoiled my night and offended Humphrey. Haven't you done well?'

Woodie had never said anything about HIV being a 'sachet of lube'. Analogies like that were much more likely to come from Elliot's fertile imagination. Still, the rest was more or less verbatim.

Blaise jostled for space on the crowded train to Edgecliff: arms and shopping bags prodded him in the side, while runaway odours from hot-cross *après*-workers mingled and mutated into something terrible – 'parfum de prole,' as Elliot would say. Blaise would never usually bother to read on the short train trip home but this time he tried, one hand gripping the warm, greasy hand rail, the other holding the book open. It was heavy in his hand and he nearly lost it with each lurch of the train. The wheels screeched beneath him, steel sparking on steel. He could feel the metal fatigue in his nerves, behind his eyes. Granville in his head. He'd removed the dust jacket. He didn't want strangers knowing what he was immersed in.

When he wasn't reading the novel, it would have to remain buried deep in his briefcase where Woodrow wouldn't see it. If Woodie snooped and discovered the book, it would serve him right.

. . . Pascal kept *Je Louse* hidden in his briefcase; he felt its weight in a way he'd never encountered with his Filofax or laptop, which were surely heavier. It weighed more than a corpse, it was heavier than an affair. Why should a grown man feel so impeded?

Pascal died inside each time he remembered the launch. Wolfgang's snide remarks to people who had been friends to both Pascal and Humphrey. Friends who admired Humphrey and saw Wolfgang as a sorry replacement, friends whom Pascal no longer felt he could see.

Why, Pascal wondered, hadn't time distanced him from Humphrey? There was no question in Pascal's mind that their grand affair was over but he'd always hoped that one day – some picture-postcard-perfect day in the future – he would be able to reminisce with Humphrey, recall the adventures they'd had together, the places they'd explored for the first time. They would sit together in an idyllic landscape with all conflicts vanquished and egos eradicated. A summer meeting in Tuscany, perhaps, or a canalside café in Amsterdam, when they were both middle-aged. Six years was its own small lifetime and those years were real; they weren't a rehearsal, however much they had seemed so at the time. Already he'd forgotten the moods, the shouting, the emotional rough and tumble that accompanies love affairs between men of disparate ages. Gone now were the final recriminations from both sides. If he weighed it all up he wouldn't swap those years for anything, and it was good and right that he remember that . . .

The train arrived at Edgecliff. Blaise felt like staying on board to Bondi Junction and riding it back, just so he had ten more minutes' reading time. It was an odd thing to do, but what the heck. Woodie would be at the gym anyhow. He felt less guilty doing it on the train.

. . . Humphrey sighed as he examined the past, his eyes looking deep into a glass of grenache for symbolic sediments, omens or clues. 'We're all blind, floundering fools, expounding our great knowledge with deluded pride over a few glasses of wine. But later, as the wine sours in our systems – sharpening the very senses we sought to dull – we weep with fear, frightened by our eternal ignorance in the bleak loneliness of the night. It is in those precise moments we are revealed and, for our revelations, reviled. All too often by those who say they love us.

Humphrey wondered if Pascal ever wept on Wolfgang's shoulder. If he did, was it seen as a weakness to be utilised in the future controlling of him? He wondered what card Pascal hadn't played yet. He'd need some cards up his sleeve with such a jealous lover, for they are always cheats. Their insecurity could swallow up the whole world, paint it a sickening, dizzy pea green if they were to let it. Humphrey hoped Pascal had kept his trump card, because the jealous lover plays from a trick pack. The trick, both nasty and ironic . . .

Blaise was back at Edgecliff station. He had to get off and shop for some dinner. Woodrow would be ready to eat the world after gym. Blaise bought pre-cut stir-fry. That way he could cook something fast. If he sat near the window, he'd be able to see the car pulling in and still have enough time to hide the book. He set his laptop on the coffee table in a pretence of work, prepared the food for cooking and delved into another chapter. He trembled as he thought what the 'nasty and ironic' trick might be, but as he began the next chapter he realised it was merely a suspense device. Neither the trick nor the irony was going to be forthcoming just yet.

. . . Lust might be the foundation, and love the house, but habit is the cement that binds it together.

Pascal snatched moments to read his forbidden book. Half an hour while Wolfgang walked the dog or exercised, extended sittings in the bathroom at work, overshooting his stop on the bus. He was sentimental and relinquished the past reluctantly. He hoped desperately for release at the end of Humphrey's book. He found it pretentious at times (as did the critics), but no one found Humphrey Calston more objectionable than Wolfgang, whose reading seldom extended beyond *BRW*. Pascal felt petty and churlish as he subtly reminded Wolfie of this literary impoverishment, but what else could he do if his lover insisted on being a book critic merely on occasions when Humphrey published a new volume? Pascal didn't think feeling proud of

Humphrey was an act of disloyalty in itself but he'd realised gradually, and rather too late, that Wolfgang was impossible about these matters. He didn't like Pascal having a past at all. What Wolfgang needed was a gay man who had gone into a coma at fifteen and woken physically perfect and virginal at thirty. The woe of it all for Wolfie was that thirty-year-old gay virgins are rare beasts indeed, and if God gave men fingers and toes to keep track of their sexual exploits, then He had underfunded the gay community rather dismally in the digit department . . .

Blaise chuckled and checked the clock. One more little bit.

. . . 'If you love something, Wolfie, you should set it free.'

'Yeah, yeah. And if it flies away it was never yours, but if it returns it's yours forever or something.'

'Exactly.'

'What about if it returns with the scent of another man's cum on its breath?'

Pascal laughed, 'I don't know, buy "it" some Listerine.'

Wolfgang didn't laugh. 'I don't know what arrangements you and Humphrey had but I saw what a mess you were when we got together, so don't tell me that the *arrangement* worked. I told you I'd never go for that sort of open-marriage shit. I'm a one-man man and you're it, baby.'

Pascal's heart sunk. How could they live amidst the

heady decadence of the city with all its booze, drugs and parties without ever slipping up – someone? Sometimes he lost Wolfie for hours at a time during Mardi Gras parties but he fought the desire to join the denizens of the grope room, as he'd so often done at Humphrey's behest. It seemed a natural desire to have these days. It was a sordid seed Humphrey had planted that would no longer have the chance to bloom, its roots twisted and crowding the pot, the flowers pale and insipid for want of sun. So he lingered faithfully in brightly lit regions where people hugged and kissed without impropriety. He thought about Wolfie, somewhere else, doing the same thing – exploring Platonic passions, not the lowly lust which so easily beckoned to Pascal these days. He danced into the lights, his eyes fixed toward the sky, sure that in denial there would be rewards, there would be something better . . .

Blaise's heart was beating fast when Woodie pulled into the garage three floors below. He pushed the book beneath the paperwork in his briefcase and set about cooking. He felt slightly aggrieved towards his lover in the same way he sometimes felt anger towards someone who'd done something horrendous and imagined in a dream but whom he still couldn't help suspecting in the waking world. It was absurd really. How could Elliot know anything about Woodie?

III

Woodrow's hair hung in bouncy ringlets. His dark eyes smouldered in the same way they had when he and Blaise had first met; he was freshly showered and powdered from the gym.

Some people are attracted to the very darkness that marks their future suffering. Blaise wondered whether he was one of *those* people. Had he sought beauty at any cost? Just what lay in the depths of those alluring pools of darkness?

'I don't know how you can bear to still be in that suit, Blaise. It's so humid. Didn't you go for a swim tonight?'

'No, I was tired.'

Woodrow blended some soy milk, bran, egg and a banana in the food processor.

'Tired – what – from sitting at your desk all day? You'll be getting love handles soon.'

He grabbed his lover's potentially handled midriff and gave it a squeeze. Blaise stir-fried, all the while repressing painful surges of anger. He was increasingly aware of Woodie insinuating cruel, personal doubts into their relationship at every possible opportunity.

'I should join your gym. I could get a lift home with you.'

'Tricky,' he said, gulping the smoothie. 'I might not go all the same nights as you, and it's a bit of a hike from Bondi Junction station. You'd do better to go to the gym at Kings Cross, then just get on the train again and you're home – easy.'

'You don't want me to go to yours?'

'I don't mind, but you know I spot with Gavin . . . I couldn't just dump him.'

'Of course not. I prefer swimming and yoga anyway.'

'Hah, when was the last time you went to yoga? And you swallow all the air you're supposed to breathe – it makes you fart.'

'I fully intend to go again, and how different are those disgusting black protein bricks you eat? They have exactly the same effect.'

Blaise finished dishing up dinner, thinking to himself: *Farting, now there's something they don't talk about on the back flap of books. 'Lectures at Princeton and UCLA, and farts in bed.' That wouldn't help sell romantic-erotic fiction, would it?* He smiled inwardly.

Woodie sat waiting for his dinner, reading the new *Bulletin* while half-watching the news.

'Hey, guess what, Blaise. Joanna at work is reading Elliot's new book. Crap with a capital C, she reckons. Full of *his* ideas on love and relationships – can you imagine!'

Blaise's eyes smarted with hot, involuntary tears. He blinked them back before Woodie caught sight. He took a deep breath as he ferried two steaming plates to the table.

'I'm not allowed to. Remember?'

'Allowed to what?'

'Imagine.'

'Why is it always a fucking drama when this comes up? I thought you'd want to know if it was crap, which I'm told it is.'

'Yeah, by Joanna, who thought *The Sweet Hereafter* was crap but *You've Got Mail* was fantastic. *Hello*. I can't even imagine why someone like *her* would read it anyway.'

'Someone gave it to her. She's a very intelligent girl, though she did say you definitely shouldn't read it and neither should I.'

'Well I would have thought that was a red rag to a bull; two bulls, in fact. Woodrow, I would so much rather make up my own mind about something like Elliot's book.'

'You are touchy, aren't you? You only call me Woodrow when you're mad.'

'What do you expect – forbidden to read my ex-boyfriend's book?'

'Forbidden? I thought we agreed it would be less distressing for you – for us, if it comes to that! Hell, me, forbid? Just don't let me see it if you succumb. I have to look at it on Joanna's desk all day, I don't want to come home to it at night as well.'

Blaise looked up from the sink. 'Let's just be thankful *he* stays in New York these days and there's no launch here – not that we'd get an invite anyway.'

'Oh drag the fucking launch up again. I apologised for that, didn't I?'

'To me, not to Elliot.'

'Blaise, I'm sure Elliot Bernard, international author, academic and wanker, has not been lying awake in bed for the last three years waiting for me to apologise.'

'I'm sure he hasn't either, but it was deeply humiliating for me. I'm going out for a walk.'

Blaise bolted out of the room, slamming the front door. Eight on a scale of one to ten. He walked all the way through Rushcutters Bay – through the Cross, got a gym application and wandered around to Potts Point, where he noticed that Clays Bookshop also had a window full of *Je Louse* with two real chalices in the display. The shop was still open, so he wandered in. He couldn't resist having a bit more of a read.

Pascal's therapist swivelled in her chair. When she wasn't looking at her patients she could look out over the harbour, the bridge, the opera house – the best of Sydney.

She twirled her pen in her mouth and Pascal wondered whether that was a habit, an oral fixation, a chink in her armour.

'Why does Humphrey's infidelity upset you so much? You don't have to stay with him.'

'I just don't understand why he does it to me.'

'Me?'

'What?'

'You said *me*. Why-does-he-do-it-to-*me*? Surely his liaisons are about doing something to himself?'

'But it affects me.'

'Yes, but it affects you if he's ill or depressed or he receives a rejection slip from a publisher. How is sex different?'

'Well, how do you think it's different? You wouldn't like it, would you?'

'We're not talking about me, Pascal. We're talking about you.'

'Well, having sex with other people is a betrayal of . . . the intimacy we share.'

'I see . . . He tells you what he's been up to, doesn't he?'

'Yes.'

'Would you rather he didn't?'

'No.'

'So it isn't betrayal that excites him?'

'I don't think so. He's often ashamed, not that it stops him.'

'I want *us* to look at what it does to *you*. Does it make you feel insecure?'

'I guess. It makes me feel like he is stronger.'

'And that bothers you?'

'I don't like being weak.'

'You don't like being weak, or you don't like feeling less powerful sexually?'

'Well . . . yes.'

'But you're attractive and quite a bit younger than him. Surely you could enjoy the same prowess if you wanted to.'

'But I don't want to put myself in that position. I don't want to get crabs or STDs.'

'So it's a hygiene issue?'

'I don't know.'

'Well Humphrey's HIV-positive and you've dealt with that for several years. Why are you scared of it outside the relationship when there is a risk within the relationship that you could become infected?'

'Well I just thought that, you know?'

'I don't know, Pascal, tell me.'

'Well, that, because I was prepared to take him on with . . . with HIV, that . . . oh, I don't know.'

'I think you do. Is it that he should play according to your rules because his value is somehow compromised by his HIV status?'

Pascal said nothing. He was pouting.

'Is that it, Pascal?'

'God, yes, maybe, how would I know?'

'Well, if that is true, it means that Humphrey has failed to live up to your expectations of how you imagine someone in his position should behave. You expect him to be more submissive – more grateful perhaps? But I think you're not looking at his position. He may see time differently with the threat that hangs over him, his age – and remember also, he has nothing to lose.'

Pascal nodded reluctantly. 'Except me.'

'Moreover, maybe you thought by confronting your fears about HIV and taking a lover who was HIV-positive, that the lesson would stop there. That you'd be rewarded.'

Pascal laughed. 'That'd be something! Humphrey, a charity case – a mercy fuck.'

He looked at his analyst. She displayed no signs of humour and Pascal, all at once, felt none himself.

'I'm afraid we're closing now. Do you want to buy that?'

Blaise felt a cold chill on a hot night. He rudely ignored the man in the shop, put the book back and kept walking. He felt alone, more exposed than the whores in the doorways, more forsaken than the drunks in the bars. *How could Elliot have come so close with the shrink? Had he told him all those things back then?* The dialogue was different, but the gist was undeniably the same. *Never share personal insights gained via psychotherapists, soothsayers or astrologers with your lover.* That would be a sturdy rule for the new millennium.

Elliot knew too much for his own, or anyone else's, good. There wasn't a single person who wouldn't know whom the book was really about. He hated Woodrow and he hated Elliot at that moment. He didn't want to go home.

IV

Woodrow rolled over and looked at the clock when he heard Blaise return.

'What's the matter with you, for God's sake?'

'I just needed to go for a walk.'

'Where did you go?'

'To the Cross.'

'And?'

'And nothing. I had a coffee and a walk.'

'You didn't go to the Pleasure Dome, did you?'

'No, I didn't go *there*. Why do you think I'd go there?'

Woodrow turned over as if he was going to sleep, but he was silently brooding. Blaise may as well have gone *there*. He may as well have gone to every sex club in Sydney for the amount of trust he got from Woodrow. Just how much of a drama would there be if he did go to a sex club, he wondered. Lately he'd felt like deceiving his lover more and more frequently. The desire for drama was overtaking him. Huge, plate-smashing dramas on a scale unprecedented in their home. But that took him back to the behavioural model he'd just read about – and experienced first-hand in the shrink's office: doing something *to* Woodie rather than taking something *for* himself. He knew from experience that infidelity for revenge was a useless and miserable course of action.

How many blood tests had he taken to prove he was negative for Woodie? Three? He'd felt like Lady Di being inspected by the royal doctors to prove herself suitably pure for Prince Charming. Woodrow made it sound like he was insisting on it for both their protection – a sensible prenuptial agreement – but really it was because Elliot's reputation preceded him. Elliot, a trailblazer for promiscuity at a time when few had the courage or stomach for it. In truth, Elliot was probably no more than a garden-variety sex junkie, an obsessive-compulsive rather than a sex radical, but nothing works like addiction when it comes to contrived rationalisations or academic gibber. Even a worm can be exquisite when perfectly rendered in the words of a poet.

All Woodie cared about was his own precious body and its enduring safety. Blaise may have been momentarily blinded by love but Woodie had pushed the love bit with that third test. He shivered as he stripped off and fell into bed. He lay with his back to his lover. He dreamt about Elliot and chains, New York and planes, ferocious dogs yapping at cars and steamy pits full of dirty sexual encounters. Elliot was smiling at him with a flute of champagne, smiling just at him – his old chum. 'We travelled far together and well, Blaise. We know each other I think from long ago. Blaise, Blaise, Blaise . . .'

'Blaise, are you getting up today or what? You'll be late.'

'Wha wha what . . . Oh Jesus, I've got a meeting at eight-thirty. Can you pour me coffee, Woodie?'

'So you're talking to me today?'

'Oh, yeah. Sorry. I'm just . . . I don't know, brain-addled.'

Blaise showered, rinsed off yesterday's anxiety, grabbed a banana and his briefcase. In a stupor, he hurried for the train.

Wolfgang's jealousy was like a kaleidoscope, a childlike thing which brought everything tumbling into its sight – blurring and mingling the whole world right before his eyes. If he turned it too fast, as he often did, the picture and planet became a nauseating carousel of paranoia. A carnival of imagined horrors and thieving souls.

If Pascal got too close to Wolfgang's friends he'd become inexplicably angry, nervous and sulky. It didn't matter whether they were women or men; Pascal's friendly charm unnerved him.

Wolfie felt even stranger with Pascal's own friends. They always referred to the past, to Humphrey. He felt they did it to rile him. Wolfgang would make sudden protests, have little ego tanties, behave oddly, drink too much and alienate people. He did it gradually, but in the end the friends placed fewer demands on Pascal, and he distanced himself because he was mildly ashamed and a little confused by Wolfie's behaviour. Wolfie in turn would criticise Pascal's friends: he branded them as pretentious, overopinionated, would-be-if-they-could-bes, so Pascal either saw them on his own or did without them completely. He felt time would help heal Wolfie of whatever childhood wounds had left him so insecure and possessive, but time passed and little changed. Perhaps the cuts were just too deep.

When Humphrey decided to go to the States and sell his flat to Pascal, Pascal needed Wolfgang's help to buy it. He couldn't afford it on his own and Humphrey offered it at a very good price, at least fifty thousand less than it would have brought at auction. To this extent, Wolfgang didn't mind living in history, although he felt it strange that Humphrey should so generously facilitate such an uncomfortable changeover. Wolfgang wasn't fooled by it, though. It was still food scraps from the enemy, piss from the past – and Wolfie never liked owing anyone anything. Pride like that finds it hard to be gracious . . .

Oh God, thought Blaise. *Could Woodrow actually be right and I'm an idiot for reading this?* He got out at Martin Place, flustered. He'd forgotten to apply antiperspirant in the morning rush and his shirt was already darkening from sweat. Elliot had made such an effort with Woodrow during the 'changeover' that Woodie deserved these criticisms, but had Blaise been so complacent himself? Should he litigate?

The morning dragged: every demand was a nuisance, every document he read, shockingly dull. Tedious caveats, boring statements and dreary testimonies. Who cared if Ms Celia Ryvitch's back fence was ten centimetres beyond where it should be on the surveyor's ordinance report? Did he care if no one had told Dr Geoffrey Biggot and his wife, Carol Biggot-Jackson, that there were plans afoot to build a motorway in the adjacent street to where they'd just bought their new home?

How was it that Blaise spent his days poring over these details while I'm-either-going-to-starve-or-write Elliot Bernard sat on his couch in Long Island with that muscle-Mary Lex and a randy bloodhound?

In Blaise's mind, Elliot was now forever frozen in that picture in *Spectrum*. Glued to that couch, eternally loved and comfortable. Allowed, by some sick prank of privileged academic justice, to work in the United States of Ambition, for God's sake. Smiling like the cat that got the cream, the girl who got the most cake, the man with nothing to lose.

He took his lunch and book to the park. He didn't want his colleagues to see him reading it, asking what it was about and whether it was any good. It was like nothing he'd ever subjected himself to before and for a moment he truly wanted to stop reading it. But Pandora's box was yawning open and nasty-ironic twists had been promised. He had to know what was inside, where all this hell might be leading to.

V

'I don't know, Humphrey. He's cute, he's hot, but it's you he's interested in, not me – not really.'

The blond boy, Drew, smiled at Pascal from the next table. Humphrey had already been talking to him, making him laugh – doing all those things he was so good at. 'Oh, he's interested in you alright. He's a honey, Pascal, let's do it. We've never done this before – not together.' Pascal looked away from the boy. He felt embarrassed – fey even. He skolled the vodka and ordered another. 'Alright, ask him over then.'

There was an uncertain silence as the three arrived back at the apartment. It was one thing to flirt in the convivial ambience of a bar but quite another to take someone home, into the sacrosanct domicile – that private domain of the couple. Drew was a little nervous, but his mischievous smile hadn't dimmed since they left the pub.

'Why don't you two get started? I've just got to do something in the kitchen.' Pascal knew that the thing Humphrey had to do was take his drugs – AZT and some of the other new ones that had engendered in his lover a sudden and rather unsettling sexual vigour. Pascal couldn't keep track of all the pills these days. He hadn't told this gorgeous Drew about that, he wouldn't mention *that* at all. That was the beauty of sex venues, it was a *caveat emptor* situation. No one asks – no one tells. *If you can't stand the heat, get out of the kitchen.* So why did Pascal feel this boy should know? Did he feel this boy should know? It's not like he had asked. Pascal felt like he was colluding in something, yet hated himself for being so uptight about it all.

'Kiss me,' said Drew.

He did. A sweet young dreamboat like that – who could resist? Drew smelt of liquor and the latest aftershave. Drew was a neat, fresh-looking guy – much more Pascal's type than the rough-and-ready street trade Humphrey usually pursued. Humphrey had hand-picked this one especially for his lover.

'I'd love to be like you guys, you know, having each other and everything.'

'Then why pick up couples, Drew, why not find yourself a boyfriend?'

'I guess I'm a voyeur, I like to see what other people

have and Humphrey, well he's quite a talker, he said you . . . I shouldn't say.'

'No, what does Humphrey say? Tell me.'

'That you love topping, you know, fucking.' Pascal cringed at the American porn lingo. He realised he was being set up as a top, and in this instance he found he didn't mind at all.

'So I suppose that means you want me to fuck you?' He caressed the boy's downy cheek as it coloured slightly in the lamplight.

'Would you?' Drew appeared coy, like a schoolboy stripped down to his underwear. Pascal looked at the exposed young man before him, amazed afresh at what gay men will do, at the intrepid nature of their lustful adventures. 'What heavenly convergences allowed such beauty to make itself so fantastically available, so poignantly vulnerable?' The miracle of it brought fire to his loins and love, of a sort, to his heart. It was good to be with someone younger for a change, to touch a different man with different smells. A boy with no traces of medication on his breath. A dish that wanted eating before it got cold.

'Oh fuck, why not.'

Humphrey entered with some glasses. 'Hey, Humphrey. I'm going to fuck Drew, what do you think about that?'

'I like it. I like it very much . . .'

'For God's sake!' It hadn't been like that, had it? How

embarrassing. How stupefyingly, horrendously embarrassing. Blaise felt sick to his stomach. His ham-salad sandwich hung limp and uneaten from his hand and now, with a painful lump in his throat, he knew he could never swallow it. 'How could he do this to me?' Tears welled in his eyes as he watched a feverishly entwined straight couple who had been at it for half an hour on the grass verge nearby.

Elliot knew that Blaise was much more coy about sex than he was – he had no right to write these scenes, however close to the truth he'd come. Elliot couldn't have known what was said if he wasn't in the room. He couldn't know all my feelings. 'Fiction, my arse!' he cried, pitching his sandwiches at some seagulls. A dark cloud rolled in abruptly, hiding the sun from the gardens. The harbour had lost its blue and a speck of rain bounced from his cheek.

'Oh God,' he moaned. 'Doesn't Elliot know that his world is different? That I'm just a legal clerk, a fruit in a suit who has to face all those queens in the very same ghetto he'd supposedly made a better place – if Blaise was seriously to believe Humphrey's launch speech. Huh – better place indeed! Write a book, piss off and leave us to stew in our juice.' He wondered if Elliot did hate him after all, but then wondered about himself and why he'd failed in the affair. Failed to do better, be happier. Because when love fails, we fail. In Elliot's words, 'When the door slams shut for the last time, the book of questions and accusations falls open and the lover must answer every one.'

Blaise went, once more, through the growing list of self-recriminations: you weren't handsome enough; not thin enough; not solid enough; not faithful enough; foolishly faithful; not honest enough; too honest by far; not clever enough; not quick enough; not intuitive enough . . . The list goes on forever, but it always boils down to the one cruel fact – you can always be a better boy. Not every good boy deserves fruit!

VI

Blaise stayed on the train to Bondi Junction – again. He might as well check out Woodie's gym, even if it was 'a hike'. He'd only ever dropped Woodie off in the car before and when he walked into the goldfish-bowl foyer he felt his usual levels of physical insecurity, testostero-anxiety and muscular intimidation. The girl at the counter looked anorexic, but the man appeared obscenely swollen and hormonally enhanced. *What a pair they made*, thought Blaise. *She's ready for hospital and he's ready for the circus*. He had the membership application in his hand, and left his briefcase at reception while he went to check out the facilities. He paused at the top of the stairs. Through a chain of reflections in the glass, he could see Woodie and Gavin exercising below. He was about to yell down to them, but paused momentarily. Gavin was doing sit-ups; Woodrow was sitting on top of his legs. He was laughing as his partner strained to sit up with a large weight clasped over his chest. He did one last heave and fell back, his face crimson.

'Fuck me!' Gavin cried in exhaustion.

'What – here?' answered Woodie, less audibly. Blaise could make out a cheeky smile on his lover's face. He was a little shocked to see Woodie being such a flirt. He hadn't seen *this* Woodrow since they'd first met.

Gavin lay back on the mat and didn't move. He just smiled up at Woodie, his face gradually resuming its normal shade. Woodie didn't take his hands from his legs, however. Instead he was stroking them – and not just the calves but all the way up, right up inside his shorts. Blaise's breath caught for a moment. He had to do a double take. Gavin lay back, pushing himself flagrantly towards Woodie's inquisitive digits, his knees now bent. The mirrors conspired to bring the reflection even closer, for Blaise's inspection. They were talking quietly. He couldn't make out what they were saying, but he could see Woodie's thumbs – and that was enough, for they were playfully fingering the elastic of Gavin's briefs, within millimetres of touching spots that have nothing to do with gym-partnering or weight-spotting. Blaise swore he could smell those musky fingers from where he stood.

He moved quickly, sneaking away like some ridiculous figure in a TV soap. His departure created a blur of motion in the reflective glass walls. Woodrow noticed a movement that drew his gaze towards the retreating figure. All he saw was the back of a suit. A creased Armani suit reminiscent of Blaise's.

VII

Fuck exercise. Fuck muscle queens and fuck Woodrow with his show-pony pectorals and nearly-but-not-quite washboard stomach. Blaise walked back through the heart of Bondi Junction and sat himself in a pub. Not a pub he'd ever been to, but a pub none the less. A table of coquettish office workers giggled and blew smoke at anyone they considered to be potential mates, while men in the sports bar watched the wrestling. Meanwhile Blaise wrestled with fumes of his own. He licked the froth from an ice-cold beer, letting the plot thicken in its own time – in his own head.

Perhaps *this* was the irony; that Woodie was in fact already playing around. Gavin had a boyfriend too. Blaise had met him. As far as Blaise knew, Gavin and his partner shared the same monogamous, imitation-hetero morality that Woodie espoused so freely and so profusely. He fingered the mobile phone as if it were the elastic on Gavin's underpants. He arrowed through the names: Aaron, Angela, Anthony, Ben, Christine, Dennis. Gavin and Rory presented itself. Would he call this Rory and share his concerns? How would it look? The frantic, neurotic voice of a cuckolded Edgecliff househusband who couldn't keep his man? Nagh. He put the mobile back in his briefcase, ordered another cold beer and reached instead for Elliot's book. A horrible nightmare that was becoming a comfort after all.

> ... Pascal went to the gym to surprise Wolfie, but Wolfie wasn't there. Wolfie hadn't been there at all that day, according to the woman on the desk. He headed home to where he assumed his lover would be waiting, but he wasn't there either. He began to cook some chicken that had been sitting in the fridge for two days. It smelt fine. But he wondered where Wolfgang could have got to. Perhaps a meeting had gone over time or a client had needed an after-hours consultation. Anything was possible, and Pascal was not unduly given to paranoia.
>
> When at last he did return, he was freshly showered, his hair still wet.
>
> 'I'm knackered,' he said, sliding into the kitchen chair and pulling his T-shirt over his head to expose a body that had not been worked-out at the gym that night.
>
> 'Where've you been?' asked Pascal. His words were soft and light.

'The gym, of course.'

But *of course* he hadn't. Pascal knew that. He said nothing; he just kept cooking, digesting this new and unpleasant revelation. His first instinct was to try and seduce Wolfgang, to force him to withdraw from a sexual scenario because he'd just had sex – with someone else. But that wouldn't work. Not any more. Pascal hadn't had that sort of power over his mate for a year, maybe more. Wolfgang would back off, pleading a defence of exhaustion or hunger. These days, sexual reluctance would prove nothing. And confrontation, well, Pascal was too tired himself to go down that track . . .

'Hooley dooley,' thought Blaise, as he drained his third schooner. He didn't want to go home but felt sweaty and drunk. He felt like asking one of the girls for a cigarette, just so Woodie would smell it on him when he got home and make a fuss. Woodie was fucking someone behind his back but wouldn't hesitate to carry on about him having a cigarette. It was all too twisted. He felt like going to one of those sex dives in Oxford Street and getting other dirty smells on him – toying with the elastic on some boy's underpants. But he wouldn't go there, not in his suit. He shoved his tie in his pocket and loosened his shirt collar, leaving a greasy stain from the packet of Kettle Chips he'd eaten. He wondered if he was getting fat and he felt his waist. He hadn't changed the notch on his belt but, as Woodie says, you get loose before you get fat Was Blaise *loose*?

'Where have you been? You look like *Death of a Salesman* and you reek of beer and smoke.'

'Just out at the pub.'

'Who with?'

'You mean with whom, don't you? Just some girls from work.'

'That sounds like fun – McCallum & Rothschild law clerks get silly on cocktails and beer.'

'I'm going out again.'

'No you're not, Blaise, you're drunk. God, look at you, you're a mess!'

Blaise was pulling off his suit. His pants dropped to the floor, his shirt made it to the laundry basket. He was a mite whiffy, he had to admit. He got under the shower and let the water take the edge off his malaise. He sang loudly as he showered '*Guess who I saw today my dear, I went in town to shop-around forrr somethin' nooo.*'

Woodie lurked, like a dark cloud, in the doorway.

'So are we going to eat?'

'I don't know. Have you cooked anything?'

'I thought you would.'

'I'm going out. I told you.'

'Where?'

'I don't know yet.'

'What do you mean, you don't know yet? I don't know what's got into you lately, Blaise, you're a nut.'

Blaise turned in the shower, his delicious eyes glittering beneath the water's crystal cascade.

'Well I know what's got into you, Woodrow, and I bet you've had *it* up to the hilt.'

'What *are* you talking about?'

'You know what I'm talking about.'

'I don't.'

'Well, when you've worked it out, let me know. It's not a trick question, darling.' Blaise continued his song, '*Ain't never bin so shocked before, I stumbled blindly for the door.*'

Woodie carried on as Blaise pulled on a T-shirt and jeans. He ranted as Blaise slung a bag containing *Je Louse* over his shoulder, and he shouted from the balcony as Blaise wandered off toward Rushcutters Bay.

Blaise found a quiet corner in the bar of the Gazebo. He wondered if Woodie would follow him; he doubted it. Woodie was definitely the sociopath in the family, but didn't they always try to project their psychoses onto their partners? Their first rule seemed to be to find a foundation of doubt and chip away at it. Blaise would not say another thing until Woodrow 'fessed-up. It would be like pulling a tooth but he'd come round in the end. Blaise wouldn't have cared so much if Woodie was honest about things, but obviously he wasn't capable of it. He assumed from what he'd seen that more than met the eye had already gone on – and anyone as jealous as Woodie would surely have to be guilty in equal part. Blaise might be getting loose but he was no fool. He opened the book. Somehow the book, awful though it was, was keeping him one step ahead in this absurd charade.

. . . Pascal loved being fucked when he was on ecstasy, in fact he loved being fucked on anything. Even the bonnet of a car. He loved to sit on Humphrey and wriggle his arse until fingers, then cock, plugged it, fulfilling some deep primal urge and enchanting lowly, sacred chakras. Often he'd straddle Humphrey and take his cock without a condom – and while it brought him hours of post-coital anguish, there were times when his desire outshone his fears about the terrible risk.

With Wolfgang it was different. Wolfie preyed on that hunger; he never said as much, but he saw it as an unmanly weakness in Pascal and played that for all it was worth in their day-to-day dynamics. He was quick to make thinly veiled references at parties that left people in no doubt about who was the top, and who the bottom. While Pascal would prefer he didn't make such comments, he didn't really feel any shame at being considered a bottom. He tended to find the whole categorisation rather tedious and patriarchal, and it gave him a great thrill when Wolfie had to swallow his macho pride and beg to be fucked from time to time. 'See, Wolfie, you're just a big old girl

too, a sissy,' he'd whisper to the assenting grunts his
partner issued during such couplings . . .

Blaise laughed, too drunk for the enormity of this particular literary betrayal to upset him. He ordered another Scotch. He'd have to go easy or he'd be too plastered to keep reading. Also, he was headed for a major hangover the next day because he'd only eaten a packet of chips.

'So which one do you identify with more, Pascal or Wolfgang?'

'What?' A man sitting on a nearby lounge had obviously read the spine of the book. He seemed every bit as inebriated as Blaise.

'I'm not sure,' said Blaise. 'Haven't finished yet.'

'There's the weirdest twist.'

'Don't tell me.'

'Oh, I wouldn't, it'd spoil it. I really liked Pascal,' the man said, nodding. 'And that thing at the party was too much . . .'

'Oh, I'm not up to the party yet, and I don't think Woodrow – I mean Wolfgang – or Humphrey are names that are in the least bit sexy.' Blaise felt like he'd walked into the twilight zone as he embarked upon this bizarre conversation. He was sure he'd seen this guy on television or something.

The man took a hefty slurp from his drink. 'A friend of mine knew him – says the whole book is based on some ex-lover of Elliot Bernard's, and Humphrey is a pseudonym for himself.'

'Really?' said Blaise, with a raised eyebrow and a legal clerk's inscrutability.

'And his real name was Bernard Elliot, can you believe?'

'Yes, I can. I studied under him.'

'No! What's he like?'

'Farts a lot.' Blaise sniggered to himself.

'What, in the lecture theatre?'

Blaise nodded. 'Foul breath, too.'

'Yuuuk,' mused the guy.

'And, a blow job at a tutorial could make the difference between a credit and a distinction.'

The man smiled. 'I bet you were the sort of student who made sure you got that distinction?'

'Oh, I worked my butt off in his tutes, but it's worse than that – his student fraternisations were nothing compared with the reasons he went to America.'

'What were they?'

Blaise lowered his voice and leaned in close to his new companion.

'He got mixed up in some exchange-student racket.'

'Racket? What do you mean?' The stooge's breath was well and truly baited.

'Oh, it was all quite sordid. He was offering these poor families in the Philippines the opportunity to put their kids through uni – a mentorship scheme, you know. He found them *benefactors*.'

'Benefactors?'

'Yeah, like patrons. Only they were really just dirty old men who were only after one thing from the students – if you know what I mean.'

'Fuck! Elliot Bernard did that? But he's always been so anti-racism and everything.'

'Well, it just goes to show: there are platitudes and there are virtues. Never the twain shall meet, I'm afraid.'

'But more should have been said about all this.'

'You're a journalist, aren't you?'

'Yes. How did you know?'

Blaise clinked the ice in his glass.

'Because journalists always think more should have been said about everything.'

He laughed. 'You couldn't substantiate any of this, could you?'

Blaise shrugged. 'This is purely off the record, you understand, but do you remember that story about a Filipino boy who drowned off some rich queen's boat at Obelisk last year?'

'Yes,' he whispered urgently.

'Well he was one of *those* students. He got a bit cocky and was threatening to make trouble. He was only fifteen when he came over and his benefactor was . . . No, I can't tell you . . . Suffice to say there were some awkward questions about his age – and frankly, none of his fields of study here were likely to lead his family back home to greener pastures, if you get my drift . . .' Blaise allowed himself an enjoyable, dramatic pause. 'His patron was panicking at the prospect of palimony, carnal knowledge and who knows what else, and the next thing we know it's "man overboard".'

The journalist's mind was ticking over, trying to piece together Blaise's audacious lies.

If there was one thing Blaise didn't mind doing, it was sullying Elliot's precious name. Elliot, the wunderkind of the Australian gay literary scene. If everyone in Sydney was going to know via *Je Louse* that Blaise could get too hot for safe sex and was basically a rapacious pig-bottom, then they should all get to hear a few nasty stories about Elliot Bloody Bernard. At that moment, Blaise wasn't at all concerned about how true the stories were.

'You remind me a little of Pascal in the book.'

'Do I? What – loose, losing my looks and unable to keep my man?'

'No, the dark eyes and big lashes – the full lips and . . .'

'Alright, alright, I get the picture. You want a shag, then?'

Blaise couldn't believe he was doing this, saying that, but it somehow made sense.

'Well, you're certainly more forward than Pascal.'

'I'm learning a lot from him . . . and in spite of him.'

'Come upstairs then. I'm staying here.'

'Why the hell not!' He drained the last of his Scotch and followed the stranger to the lift. He'd always had a soft spot for the Gazebo, or the 'Gay's a bow' as taxi drivers seemed to call it. The soft spot was now hardening.

Blaise decided not to shower after the sex (it was fast, trashy sex, which was exactly the sort he'd needed). Neither was he going to stay and get caught up in endless dissections of *Je Louse*. He wanted the smell of someone else to linger on him for when he finally got home and collapsed into bed next to Woodrow. He hoped his lover would notice the smell. He'd wave his fingers casually in front of Woodie's untrusting nose and then deny the smell belonged to someone else. After all, that's what his lover was doing to him. The whole charade was appalling.

But he wasn't ready for home yet. He went into a café for coffee, his head thumping a little now from sex, booze and the amyl bottle that had been thrust under his nose at a particularly opportune moment during the encounter. He ordered cake, pleased to be doing completely different things from his usual, predictable repertoire. He was miserable, of course, but there was something liberating in the misery. He could ponder the way ahead over his cake and coffee. He could trawl the streets all night and get into who-knew-what sorts of trouble. He smelt his index finger as he sipped from the cup.

'Anything else, love?'

'Yes.' He pointed at the lady with the same finger, then directed it at the counter.

'Some sugar, please.'

> ... Pascal felt exposed, totally naked like some frightened waif being paraded past all Oxford Street's scene queens. 'How could Humphrey have done this?' he pondered over a Long Island tea he could barely wade through. This final drink had come at the end of what was shaping up to be quite a bender. All those queens with their makeshift morality – Friday night's virgins, Sunday night's sluts. The humidity was bad enough, but the closeness of the city was insufferable. He could choke on it – just as Humphrey had choked on all those disembodied cocks shoved at him through dirty glory holes in shabby porn lounges. At least Humphrey had abandoned himself to it, gone to hell in a hand-basket, as he put it. Pascal might have seen the tears from Humphrey's remorse, but he never doubted the recidivism they tried to mask ...

He couldn't read any more, he was physically unable to. He was smashed. Back on the street, a seedy man with a cloak-and-dagger voice offered him heroin – one pleasure he had decided to postpone until he was terminally ill. A prostitute with splayed legs poked at the dirty gusset of her panties while a bikie urinated all over the ATM. 'Oh yes, I'm back in the real and dirty world now,' thought Pascal, as a Tarot card woman touted for customers from a makeshift stall in front of Crazy Prices Everyday. He plonked himself down on a foldaway chair and placed a scrunched-up twenty-dollar bill on her foldaway card table.

'The cards or the palm, laddie? The choice is yours.'

She pocketed the cash while he proffered a hand. He was too drunk to comprehend the slapping and moving about of cards, much less shuffle them himself.

'Someone's been up to no good, if you'll follow me.'

'ME?' cried Blaise, too quickly and defensively.

'I didn't say who it be. The curly-haired one's not worth tuppence. He'll make a devil of you before you'll an angel see in him ... Who's that?' she gushed, a scowl descending upon her craggy face.

'Who's who?'

'An American, something about America. A dirty sod. Says you're an artist, but you've no such thoughts of it yerself ... a poet, if you'll believe it.' She cackled wildly.

'What about my job?'

'Nothing'll come of it. Is it the courts, government?'

'Law, yeah.'

'You'll never make a lawyer. Best follow the American, though 'e's strange an' all,' she continued cackling.

'What, follow him? *Go* to him?'

She was laughing harder now, shaking her head – as if in disbelief at what tales lay hidden before her in the creases of his palm.

'Well you won't do badly out of it if ye do, and

buzzards'll claim the rest.' She'd lost interest now and returned to mundane revelations about career. 'Follow his advice. Be an artist, you'd do better as *that.*'

She was pointing at some scruffy street artist who was selling lurid portraits of Sydney Harbour and the Opera House from a section of pavement he'd claimed for a stall. Ghastly pictures surrounded him, with explosions of fluorescent colour signifying fireworks or plump caricatures of koalas and garish cockatoos with sloppy yellow slashes for crests.

He wanted to know more. What were the buzzards? He looked at the desperately scrawny man painting the pictures; a limp fag-end was dangling from between the man's lips. The fortune teller would say no more, she'd done with him now. The artist was winking at Blaise, and a prostitute whose heel had snapped off her shoe was trying to hammer it back on with the end of a beer bottle. A nightmare.

VIII

Woodrow paced and fidgeted. Woodrow ate a can of beans and left the remains in the sink. And ultimately Woodrow's thoughts turned to the copy of *Je Louse* he had secreted at the bottom of his gym bag. He'd swiped it from Joanna's desk because she'd flown off to Melbourne for a conference. She wouldn't be back for four days, so he had plenty of time to see what all this rubbish was about.

Blaise was impossible, unstable, weak – and not really what Woodie had hoped for in a relationship. Blaise was a poor thing, but his own. It had been different when Blaise was with Elliot; guys used to be really hot for him then. He seemed confident and mature, but sexy and young at the same time. Woodie stroked his chest and stomach. Smooth and fit. Blaise didn't keep himself in good enough shape, that was half his problem. 'It's funny how sometimes you get really attracted to people when they're involved with someone else,' Woodie thought. 'But when you get them for yourself, you kind of realise how corrupt they are.' Woodie knew that if Blaise could be tempted away from Elliot, he could just as easily be unfaithful now. He found that kind of knowledge hard to live with, especially when he knew the sort of filth Blaise had probably been a party to with Elliot. Still, there was the flat to consider – that was a definite gain he'd made over the last three years.

People like Elliot Bernard gave homosexuals a bad name. Woodie hated all those arty, foppish types Blaise used to hang out with. If gay men could learn to behave in a cooler, straighter way, then perhaps it would be safer on the streets for all of us. All those prissy, loudmouthed queens did nothing but stir up hatred and violence. Besides, Woodie didn't need to listen to the pretentious crap they came out with.

Gavin at least understood some of those things. He was more of a man's man. His boyfriend was a flight attendant who was away a lot, so sometimes he and Gavin fooled around. Gavin was really clean and safe. The only reason they'd been mucking about at all was because they had a really intense connection – when that happened, it was out of your control. It was as if God or the cosmos just handed you a gig and you had to play. Sometimes you just met someone like that and whatever anyone else might say, it was a far cry from those filthy sex dens Elliot and Blaise used to go to. Some things were written in the stars, and what certain people didn't know couldn't hurt them.

For Woodie, sex was really about a man being with another man – not a queen, faggot or some drug-fucked disco twinkie. Gavin understood that. He really fought to be the *man*, to stay on top; he'd put on quite a show. 'No way are you fucking me, man, 'til I've got my end into you.' Woodie fought too, of course, wrestled for power on Gavin and Rory's bedroom floor but, in the end, that was the way it was for Gavin. With Blaise it was kind of boring these days – Blaise still trying out that cutesy thing, which may have worked when he was twenty but didn't work now, or at least not for Woodrow.

Woodie didn't want to hurt Blaise with all this affair shit. It wasn't even an affair really – just a guy thing, but also a spiritual thing. You couldn't explain that kind of feeling, so it was better not to try. It just happened from time to time with some guys, guys who just *knew* each other intuitively; it wasn't a soft-cock poofy kind of thing like it had gotten to be with Blaise. Still, it wouldn't do for Blaise to know about it. If he did, he'd get it into his head that it was OK to go to saunas and God knows where else. Woodie did not approve of those places and would not have his health put at risk by a lover who traipsed around them like a piece of trash. He definitely didn't want to suffer the humiliation of people he knew gossiping that they'd seen Blaise hawking his stuff at those clubs. Woodrow was too noble for that.

Woodie already knew from the stories about Elliot just how addictive that sort of behaviour could be. Blaise had told him about it in the early days – he used to laugh about it. 'Can you believe Elliot would go to three or four of those clubs in one night, Woodie?' And Woodie had trouble believing it. He'd shake his head in disgust, frightened that Blaise could have accepted that sort of thing, wondering what sort of sick spell that filthy old slut had cast over Blaise to make him incapable of leaving.

It was Woodrow who'd moved in – saving Blaise from a shocking situation, from a fate worse than death. The shame of it all was that Blaise had never realised just how lucky he'd been to find Woodrow, and with each new book written it was as if Elliot Bernard was recasting his depraved hex. Woodie shook his head sadly, 'And what with all this bloody combination therapy – it was really nothing more than a licence to the Elliot Bernards of this world. They broke the laws of nature once and now science had found a way for them to do it all over again. Dangerous chemically reanimated Lazaruses carrying viral-load time bombs.

And what the fuck was happening now? What sort of *episode* was Blaise having? Going out drinking, reeking of cigarettes and wandering off to the Cross on his own. Perhaps the damage had already been done. Perhaps once a monster like Elliot lured a disco dolly like Blaise into a life of vice – that was it. Kapputto. Still, there was one bit of dirt Woodrow had on Elliot. One dark little secret that really showed Elliot for what he was. Woodrow had Elliot's number. He knew him and he knew his type.

Woodie wondered if that suit he'd glimpsed in the gym had been Blaise's. He was probably just being paranoid. Besides Blaise said he'd been drinking with the girls from work, and he certainly smelt like it. He shook his head at the pity of it all. That he, a man in his physical prime, should end up a wet nurse to a very damaged young man. He looked in the mirror and licked his lips. 'Not really even a *young* man any more. And where the fuck was he, anyway? He flopped onto the bed, determined to see just how crappy this book was. He opened to the first page.

What are you reading, honey?

IX

It's not a good place to cry, Kings Cross. Not that people don't; they do all the time, but Blaise liked to think that those who did were much more disenfranchised than himself. He knew he was drunk and he did cut quite a tragic swath in the landscape of the night but he hoped he was acutely tragic, not chronically so. He felt like a joke, and on that thought he issued a single macabre laugh which involuntarily turned into a sob.

He sat in a bar on Darlinghurst Road – a bar he'd passed a million times, but not the sort of beer barn any self-respecting Sydney homosexual would ordinarily go into. It was a glassed-in joint frequented entirely by drunks, down-and-outs and bewildered tourists who were unaware of anywhere better to go. A woman in a tracksuit who looked like a truck driver jammed an ashtray into the pay-out tray of her poker machine. 'Don't even think about it,' she waved a chubby finger at him. 'Me luck's nearly in,' she shouted as she ventured off for more change.

'Whata bout cha?' said a drunken Irish man next to him.

'What about me?' said Blaise, as the threat of sobs receded again.

'Have ya been to Sydney before then?'

'Before when?' Blaise was confused.

'Is it cha first time?'

'Oh, yeah.' He meant *yeah* to convey that he understood, but now he'd started something else.

'So where ya from?'

'Noo York.' He adopted the accent in the nick of time.

'Ah, Ireland's other capital.'

'Sure is, Italy's and Israel's too.'

'Can I get you a beer, or is it a Guinness you'd be wanting?'

'Oh, a regular beer would be fine.'

Blaise thought about another beer. There was now beer, potato crisps, Scotch, coffee, cake and more beer in his gut. It was a disgusting thought, but it was such a rough bar that he thought it might start a brawl if he dared order anything but beer. He excused himself to go to the toilet and snuck out onto the street. He searched in his wallet for a credit card, bought a half bottle of whisky and checked into a sleazy dive complete with a flickering neon sign.

He wasn't going to ring home. Every hour he was away would conjure myriad jealous fantasies for Woodie: *Blaise in the sling being fucked by a queue of faceless slavering men; Blaise shagging cuter, younger boys than Woodrow; shirtless Blaise at the centre of a dance floor with clusters of gorgeous men licking his nipples as shards of refracted light beamed from his delirious eyes. Ah yes, all sorts of men offering him drugs and promising sensational bedroom adventures that would last until dawn.* Blaise felt himself swoon at the many possibilities, but knew he didn't have the mettle or stomach for any of it tonight.

He looked at the phone and thought of Elliot. He wondered if he could dial direct from such a hotel. He picked up the receiver. Elliot had emailed him the number a year previously. He'd never dialled it before, but he'd committed the number to memory long ago: 0011 to get out of Australia, 1 for the USA, 516 for the area, and then the seven-digit number. Blaise marvelled at his extraordinary mental recall. He listened for the telltale 'bibalibalib' and felt the anxious thrill of leaving Australia – his message conveyed by satellite to the other side of the planet. He could picture the phone ringing. He wondered if the handset was right beside the cream couch he'd seen in the newspaper photo, with the Keith Haring painting behind it. He wondered if it was a print or an original. He wondered whether Glasnost was allowed on the furniture and whether at that precise moment Elliot and Lex were having ribald penetrative sex. He felt a sickening twinge of complicated lust at the thought. The phone kept ringing as he speculated what spring would be like on Long Island, and how they could possibly afford to live in a huge house there. He dreamt of turning up on the doorstep and seducing Lex Fucking Constantine. He wondered if Lex was one of those good, clean, earnest American types who couldn't easily be tempted into betraying his lover, and whether Elliot had or hadn't changed his filthy ways since he'd arrived in the States. Who could say?

'Hello . . .'

Blaise was silent. 'Hello . . . is anybody there? . . . José, is that you again?'

Blaise felt his heart stop for a second as he listened to what must have been Lex's voice. He wondered if he could pull something off. He couldn't do it for long, not with the time delay – and God knows what José sounded like.

'Yeah, it's me.'

'You don't sound so good.' Lex sighed. 'I asked you not to call me here . . . I've said all I have to say, do you understand?'

Blaise hung up the phone. His heart was racing. The drama was not only international but uni-bloody-versal. Long Island, Schlong Island.

X

'The arsehole, the evil fucking bastard,' yelled Woodrow, ready to fling the book across the room before he remembered it belonged to Joanna. No way was he buying another copy of this. He wasn't throwing five cents' worth of royalties in Elliot Bernard's direction.

. . . Wolfgang was a *pique-assiette*; he stole from the plates of others. In a restaurant he would choose not by looking at the menu but by peering at other diners' dishes when they emerged from the kitchen. 'I'll have what he's having.'

As a child he would have desired his sibling's presents over his own but even his insecurities were never that static. With mental disorders there is medication but for jealousy, nothing. Just endless rows, nasty transparent games and, ultimately, violence . . .

Woodrow grunted. It was past two a.m. and he was still reading. He had work tomorrow and that piece-of-shit-Elliot had him fretting over this rubbish.

And as for *violence*! He'd only ever hit Blaise twice, and he'd been drunk both times. Just a brisk smack across the face – and not in front of anyone else. Blaise used to literally hang off his friends. Hugging and kissing them like some prissy nineteen-year-old. He only did it to wind up Woodrow. Twice he'd slapped him, before Blaise said that if it ever happened again, it was all over. Well, Woodie never had done it again. There are much more subtle ways of controlling your partner's idiotic ways than a whack across the face. With a quick smack though at least it's honest, you know where you stand. And it's over. The pressure subsides.

Woodie wondered if perhaps Blaise had been reading *Je Louse* too. That would go some way to explaining his extraordinary behaviour of late, but staying out all night was pushing it too far. He must be *with* someone. Woodrow went to the cupboard in search of a Valium or something. There was no way writing a book like Elliot's could possibly be moral and he was already wondering if it was legal. This sort of libellous stuff was why we had lawyers – and if Elliot Bernard's way of getting to be a big, fat, rich pig was by ruining other people's lives then it was about time something was done. As he read on, he even began to feel protective of Blaise, though some of the explicit intimacies described raised other questions. Questions which could have impacted on his own health:

> . . . Pascal had an almost marsupial mode of seduction. It started out all cute 'n' cuddly but turned very savage, very fast. Kissing you and wetting you, moving down to the cock and formatting it with his mouth for another cavity.
>
> 'You're not wearing a condom, are you, Humphrey?'
>
> 'I'm just putting one on now.'
>
> 'Don't!' Pascal's voice sounded like the Devil's own in the darkened bedroom. Nothing but the buzz of sexual possibility could be felt in their intimate space, and Humphrey paused as if the voice of the Devil was the sweet voice of God.
>
> 'You've got the Devil in you tonight, Pascal.'
>
> 'God, the Devil . . . don't you know they're the same thing? Two ends of the same stick, now give me yours!'
>
> 'I don't like to, baby. You know that freaks me out.'
>
> But it didn't matter whether Pascal knew that or not. He was sliding back onto his lover's cock, a cock that had hardened even more with this new, forbidden development . . .

'Oh God!' cried Woodrow, his mind ready to snap. 'Who's to say any of this is true anyway? It's only a novel, for Christ's sake, it doesn't claim to be true. But why a name so similar to mine? Pascal could be anyone, but *Wolfgang* – I'm not paranoid. God, tell me I'm not paranoid.' The only way Woodie would ever know was to read on.

He tried to read ahead; he tried to find the future passage he was already dreading. He hadn't been able to locate the notorious party, nor the specific incident, but the bastard had hinted at it, tortured Woodie with the promise of something nasty. 'If Blaise read that . . . Oh God, it didn't bear thinking about' – and on that depressing note he began to feel the dulling brainwaves from the sedative. He took a drink of Scotch with him to bed. If Blaise wasn't there, who was to know about his lapse? He was worried about Blaise. Really worried. He loved that little marsupial, that glittery-eyed fella he'd been with for years. But even love had rules, and Blaise had agreed to play by them a long time ago.

XI

Blaise woke at nine, head thumping – mouth foul. He had a real beery, yeasty, nasty hangover, but not enough to make him sick. The alarm hadn't gone off at seven. They never do in those sort of hotels. He'd set it in the unlikely event that he might attempt to go home, change and get to work on time. Now he would ring in sick, go home and read the dreaded book all day until he had to confront his partner. He'd need to ring Woodie at work and tell him he was home, in case he tried to reach Blaise at the office.

He couldn't believe he'd phoned Elliot. *And what was that thing with Lex about?* Blaise was really in the cuckoo zone now. The hotel room smelt grotty. Years of fornication and cigarettes. Somehow he hadn't noticed its rare bouquet the previous night when he checked in.

The establishment itself was only a marginal step up from the kind rented by the hour to prostitutes and their clients. People at least stayed the whole night here. He could make out dirty footmarks at strange angles on the walls. What the previous inhabitants had got up to was anybody's guess. An air conditioner that had infiltrated his dreams with its noise still shuddered away in the window, while a German couple bickered at each other in the next room.

He thought about the journalist he'd had sex with. How business-like and dirty it had all been, yet how fulfilling. It occurred to Blaise that gay men over the age of thirty often negotiated sex as casually as a game of pool. He wondered why in bars people didn't just go over and place two dollars in front of the trade of their choice.

'At this point in time,' he pondered, 'I could manage sex with Elliot even though I hate him. Why would I desire something so obviously humiliating and self-destructive?' He even thought he might get that video of Elliot's and have a watch while Woodie was at work. 'But Woodrow, urrghh. I've gone completely off him, which is probably just as well because he hasn't shown the slightest interest in me lately.'

Blaise wondered why everyone was under so much pressure to be in a perfect relationship. You had to be attractive, thin, healthy and wealthy. You needed a good job, a bright social life and when you returned home to your lover of however many years it would be hammer 'n' tongs action all night long. Happy couples, schmappy couples.

At home a telltale mess of dishes were resting in the sink. An ugly protest at Blaise's absence. He rang Woodie, who was not a happy chap at all.

'Where the fuck are you?'

'At home. I'm sick . . .'

'In the head. What are you up to, Blaise? I'm not going to take much more of this, you know.'

'I've had enough, Woodrow.'

'Enough what?'

'Of you.'

'Oh, and you're so easy to live with.'

'I'm not even *here* any more. I don't even exist.'

'What are you on about *now*?'

'All I have managed to become, Woodie, is a wound-up bunch of responses to your neuroses. A psych nurse trying to second-guess your episodes and stay one step ahead. You have swallowed *me* up with all your insecurities. People used to like me once.'

'You mean people used to pretend to like you because you were Elliot's boyfriend.'

'No, they did like me. You won't convince me otherwise – not this time. You're always trying to chip away at my self-esteem. I'm over it.'

'It's only a novel, Blaise.'

'What?'

'*Je Louse.*'

'You wish it was, don't you? Are you reading it too?'

'I just had a look at Joanna's.'

'Well, when I come across something in there which I think is fiction, I'll let you know.'

'If that shit Elliot has used us to write a book, Blaise, we can sue him for slander or libel, or whatever the fuck that thing is.'

'To do that, Woodie, it would first of all have to be untrue. Then we'd have to prove it was about us.'

'I never said some of those things, like HIV being a sachet of lube for his debauchery and stuff like that.'

'Believe me, Woodie, we don't have the money to make a case – and so far as I've read, *you* don't have a leg to stand on.'

'But all that unsafe sex stuff! He had no right to say that about you. Surely you're furious. You wouldn't have got into stuff like that, Blaise – you've got more sense. We should stop reading it – look at what it's doing to us! He's sick.'

'No, Woodrow, he's alive and well and living on Long Island with his playwright boyfriend and a bloodhound called Glasnost.'

XII

... Pascal sat with Tammy in a Balmain café. It would be the last time they went out for one of their intense chats. In the old days, a week didn't go by without Pascal and Tam doing coffee or cocktails or a night on the tiles. They'd been inseparable since puberty.

'I always think it's strange,' Tammy sighed, as she rolled a cigarette from her little 1920s tin of tobacco.

'What's strange?'

'How brilliant, shiny people with loads of potential never rub off onto their partners. It always seems to be the other way around.'

'What's the other way around?'

'Well, when people are weak and insecure – even mean – and they're in a relationship with a brilliant-shiny, they always drag the shiny down. You see it all the time.'

'Are you saying that about people in general or about someone specifically, Tam?'

'I dunno.'

'You're talking about Wolfie and me, aren't you?'

'I never mentioned names, did I? God, you're starting to sound as paranoid as him.'

'It seems to me like my little group of friends have already had their grand court case – the verdict is well and truly in, and Wolfgang's out.'

'What do you expect us to say – me to say. He's a boor, he keeps you on such a short leash I can't even see the chain any more. I love you, Pascal, but it is totally and absolutely beyond me how you could go from Humphrey to . . . *that* in the space of six months. The most painful thing is you can't even see what's happened. You're like one of Pavlov's dogs.'

Pascal laughed dismally. 'Now we've enshrined Humphrey, have we? Humphrey, lost somewhere between the dogma of his own ego and the glittering towers of New York's publishing houses. Alright, I'm Pavlov's dog, Humphrey's dog; beg for Humphrey, jump for Humphrey, sit on Humphrey's bone. Well maybe that's – all – I – fucking know, Tammy. Woof woof.'

'Oh, don't be so bloody melodramatic. You're pushing thirty now, you're no one's toy boy any more, the whole world doesn't go weak at the knees every time you wiggle your tush, and you're grown up enough to know what's good for you. I always admired you, Pascal, but I don't any more, can't any more . . .'

Tammy had to be Teresa – and in reality she'd never been quite that confrontational. She'd pleaded with her eyes, said too much after too many drinks and finally stopped phoning him altogether, but if she read *Je Louse* she wouldn't think that Elliot was too wide of the mark. In fact all of *them* were probably having a ball reading the fucking thing. The thought made Blaise feel even worse. A poor lost love, a laughing-stock. And a Pavlov's dog to boot. He was trembling like a puppy, as discomfort crept over him like a rash. He had nowhere to hide, and even Woodie's attempts at colluding with him over the whole malodorous thing merely made his flesh crawl.

He flicked to the end. He had eighty pages to go. For a short-lived objective moment, he suspected he might be bored with the book by now, were he not the star of the show. Somewhere in another book he'd read a line that went: '. . . the couple shared their silver anniversary and the prize for their endurance was a hatred that nothing short of twenty-five years could have purchased.' He'd thought it cruel and cynical, even as it rang true. Was that what he was pursuing? Hatred. If things were bad now, they would only get worse. Why did everyone coo over lengthy relationships – especially gay ones? Was the quantity of time really so much more important than the quality? It was as if sometimes the cosmos got bored with the tedious bickering of everyone's codependency, it groaned, shuffled everything around and made sure you had to move on, no matter how scared and neurotic you were at the thought.

He had hoped desperately as a teenager that his own mother would leave his stepfather, a man in whom Blaise had never found any merit. His mother had simply said, 'When you're my age, you'll understand how limited my choices are. Maybe as a man you'll never have to know.' It sounded absurdly defeatist to him. 'The lesson, darling, is make the right choice the first time.' Yet here he was, imprisoned at thirty. Surely his choices weren't all used up yet; she'd been a good fifteen years older than he was now when she was hatching such dire epithets.

'The honey-tree of youth, each sweet drop that drips, suckled by famished admirers, an eager mating place for busy bees. Yet when the honey runs out, the branches are bare and few seek its shade and nectar.' Bloody Humphrey and his florid metaphors. Blaise had never cared for them that much, yet they ran through his head at times as if he'd learnt the books by heart. It was only *Intra Venus* that he'd read three times, the dedication burnt into his memory: 'For the Blaise in my heart, a furnace of love that never dwindles.'

But dwindle it had, and he'd be a fool to think otherwise. They were mere words. They were said, but they're done with now. Blaise needed all the pride he could garner if he was to continue facing the story before him. Tears welled up again as he realised that Elliot could not have really loved him and written such an exposé. Was he so desperate for another bestseller that he was hawking his soul, 'my soul, the secrets we had shared'. Was this his *In Cold Blood*? And where to from here – commit a murder just to have done it? Writers, skiters.

XIII

... Humphrey had never previously smuggled drugs into Australia, so when he arrived at Sydney airport and actually saw the dogs being led out by customs officials, his pulse quickened. His facial expression, however, remained impassive and no beads of sweat leavened his brow.

He had double-wrapped a balloon filled with various high-grade, New York party tricks inside two condoms. Just before the aircraft began its descent, he had inserted them in his anus, an anatomical aperture that, given the puissant exploration it had withstood over the years, seemed to have expanded into a veritable tardis. He hoped its appearance was still discreet enough that it would cause no immediate alarm, should customs employees dare to strip-search him and interrogate any such chasms of doubt ...

'Oh, fucking disgusting,' Woodie muttered to no one in the empty work cafeteria.

. . . 'Mardi Gras may be the best one yet,' he thought. With this tidy stash, he could likely lure all the men of his choice back to his suite with the creamy promise of precious milk from the nipple of America's underbelly. And don't those gorgeous boys go silly for it all? Those ten cents a dance days were definitely over for Humphrey. And, with such a diverting bounty on board, he doubted anyone would notice the four kilos he'd discreetly gained since his last visit.

He hadn't arranged to see Pascal. It was probably best not to, though he had emailed him details of his hotel should he wish to get in contact himself. Mardi Gras was such a crazy time that even Pascal and Wolfie might find themselves separated for several hours, and Humphrey thought that would be the best time to bump into his ex. He, like most people, preferred Pascal on his own.

Poor Humphrey had learned the hard way that while success may outwardly increase one's desirability, it ultimately reduced one's lovability. Regardless of whether success was in fact talent, a gift from the gods or merely the machinations of a publisher's marketing machine, sooner or later its subject would swell and corrupt with the egotism it bestowed. From then on, spontaneous, naïve, romantic love would become a treasured memory from a halcyon past. A dreamily remembered state, with all the inherent flaws carefully edited out.

God, couldn't some of this have been edited out? mused Woodrow, as he devoured his protein block. *Was there no end to Elliot's egotistical yabber?* Still, Woodie was in no hurry to get to the party scene that he knew must be lurking somewhere in the pages, no hurry at all. If Blaise was at home he'd probably get to it first, and that wasn't a thought he relished either.

Gavin would be at the gym, and he felt better about *their thing* now. He couldn't believe for one minute that Blaise had stayed out all night without getting up to something, and his blood boiled at the thought. If Blaise thought he was going to get one bit more of that flat than he was strictly entitled to, he had another think coming. If he wanted to go crazy all of a sudden, then he could do so elsewhere. Woodie had to remember not to get aggro. With all those legal ponces Blaise knew, violence could make material things tricky if their marriage really was on the rocks. He had to read on though. He had to know where he stood in this story.

XIV

. . . The annual buzz of speculation about which artists would be performing at the Mardi Gras party was an easy source of poolside chat: Madonna, Jimmy Somerville, Kylie Minogue, Chaka Khan, Marcia Hines. It was the same every year, and the rumours doubtlessly originated from the Mardi Gras factory itself. Humphrey sat with a handsome, black Californian, his female model friend, a sultry English lad with his slightly older lover, and several Australian blow-ins from a mess of different cities. He'd never met any of them before, but Mardi Gras seemed to foster an international camaraderie that never failed to delight Humphrey.

'I have a friend at Qantas who can do passenger searches, and she reckons there's definitely no Madonna on any of their flights or with any affiliated airline,' said a Melbourne boy.

'God,' sighed the American, 'I can't imagine *her* flying United; they'd have to book out the entire first class. The goddess couldn't travel with regular folk. Surely she'd have a private flight, the Madonna Special. What about RuPaul?' The American and the model launched into a little Madonna-meets-RuPaul dance routine.

'I don't think Mardi Gras could afford Madonna, somehow,' muttered Humphrey over the top of his drink. 'I've heard it's Jimmy but I'm sworn to secrecy. I'm only telling a few dozen of my closest friends.'

Everyone giggled.

'I've some champagne and other delights in my room, if you'd all care to join me.' And it seemed the Pied Piper had struck a note to which all the children might dance, as the exuberant convoy of hedonists followed him to his twelfth-floor suite . . .

Blaise could certainly picture Elliot poolside, though he thought him an unlikely candidate as a drug importer. But who knew what sorts of risks his ex-lover might take these days? Blaise would have killed him if he'd ever attempted such a thing in his company. But as Blaise contemplated this thought, he reminded himself that nothing engendered deceit as much as forbidding. *In fact*, thought Blaise, *the rules a partner laid down were probably the most provocative of all. Just like parents' rules – you wanted to break them. You wanted to prove that no one could control you, that no one's will could be imposed on your own.* He felt a chill at the truth of it.

Suddenly he realised how desperately he longed to disobey all the rules he had agreed to with his own lover. Rules, fools.

... Humphrey looked at the two English men. Much to his surprise, the older one, Calvin, interested Humphrey more than the younger, cuter partner. He proffered a straw so his companion could hoover up another line of some very fine Miami coke. Calvin leered at him pleasantly; it wasn't a hungry leer just yet. Humphrey was lost in a moment of depraved calculation. What exactly would be involved in having this man betray his lover? What circumstances might conspire to leave them alone together just long enough for such a betrayal to take place? He was overcome momentarily with the will to move heaven and earth in order that his desires might be met – he had done as much in the past. His soul sighed with the magnitude of guilt he was busy purchasing. He knew English boys could be tricky as far as such contrivances were concerned but then he knew the whole world could become sharp-edged and savage when deceit was on the drawing board.

'All dynamics are mere contrivances,' he sighed to himself. 'They've come here to party, and party they shall. If they'd truly wanted to stay sheltered and fey in some tenement in Manchester, Birmingham, or wherever the fuck they said they were from, then they should have stayed there. But they're here, snorting my drugs and enjoying my risqué hospitality – what else can they expect?'

The black Californian and the model were giggling with Calvin's boyfriend and the glances that were emanating from him were more akin to the sad, jaded 'This sort of thing has happened before' than 'Sod off or I'll fuckin' doof ya.' Besides, Humphrey felt obscenely confident with the drugs pulsing through his system. Humphrey was used to having things go his own way . . .

Blaise grunted. Humphrey was turning out to be worse than Elliot. Humphrey (if such a beast existed) was a torture to us all. 'Do some people have so much power? Can some people always get what they want?' Blaise felt exhausted by Elliot's lust. Suddenly he wished Elliot was ten years older, so all his sleazing and carousing could finally be laid to rest. If not that, then at least he would be reduced to nothing more than a dirty old man, a reptilian creature with darting eyes and hopeful glances. As it was he was still producing this lust, this endless quest that was as impossible as it was insatiable. Blaise wondered why he felt so uncomfortable about that. Perhaps that's all Elliot was: desire. 'What would it matter if it were true? Would the world end? Would the stars fall from the sky?' No, it was just Blaise. Blaise feeling needy and insecure – all the emotions he'd never shaken off. Blaise feeling the sum of things that had allowed him to be so easily left behind for someone bigger, someone better, someone younger. Someone else. He had to remind himself from time to time that it was he who left Elliot. If only Elliot had left him, then he could enjoy his natural victim disposition so much more.

X V

. . . 'Can you stand it, Wolfie? I mean, can you stand the excitement?' crooned Pascal from the bathroom.

'You just can't wait to see all those near-naked men, can you?'

'And that will be hard for you, I suppose?'

'I'll cope.'

'Of course you will, you're the one who spends all your time at the gym so boys will look at you. I'm happy with my underdeveloped, pizza-eating, swimmer's body.'

'You shouldn't be so blasé, Pascal.'

'What can I say? I'm a face man.'

Pascal was sculpting his hair with a range of cementing products and polishing his face with pricey creams, while his lover lifted dumbbells in the bedroom to effect that last-minute pumped-up look.

'Tammy says we homos are too narcissistic. She reckons we are looking for our reflection so we can mate with it. Virtual masturbation, she calls it.'

'Tammy's full of shit and smokes too much dope. She's looking for a gay man to fuck so she won't have to deal with straight insensitivity.'

'Well how come every couple at your gym are exactly as sculpted as each other. They all have the same haircuts too. It's like the Patty Duke Show on testosterone in there. Kissin' cousins. I bet their farts even smell the same.'

'Well that'd be about your level, Pascal. Farts. It's always the guys that don't got *it* who criticise them that do. It's always fat women who go on about thin women being oppressed. Don't you ever think there's something going on there? I'd rather be envied and oppressed than be 120 kilos of liberated fat and sitting by the phone. If you don't appreciate my body, I'm sure there are plenty of others who would.'

'Yeah, but would they put up with the moods?'

Pascal wasn't usually so frank but he'd had a couple of lines of speed. Wolfie wasn't usually so tolerant but then he hadn't started drinking yet. Pascal knew his comments could come back to haunt him later in the night. If things didn't go really well, if Wolfie ended up more drunk than drug-fucked, their Mardi Gras could well be marred by a nasty early-morning exchange and one of those self-same moods he'd just mentioned.

Wolfgang's moods were like summer storms, oppressive and pervasive. One of his moods filled the entire apartment, and would cover the whole world if atmospheric conditions were favourable. Their home just wasn't big enough for Pascal, Wolfie and one of his moods. Pascal could see the pattern for the night emerging: the digs, the jibes. Even the ecstasy failed to bring back the illusion of the ardour they once shared. Pascal thought about the declarations he'd made at the beginning of the affair. Where did the energy for such undying declarations come from, and how could it dissipate so? . . .

There was no one else left now, just Woodie reading alone under the glare of the canteen fluoro. He was sick of reading, tired of Elliot and his endless ramblings. Woodie never wanted to be gay. He didn't want to belong to some social underclass with morals and practices that were no better than those of dogs in the street. He hurled the can of Diet Coke he'd been drinking at the wall, and ruefully watched the brown tears trickle down the notices stuck there. *Why couldn't people just fucking shut up about what they'd done?* It had almost been an accident, after all.

XVI

. . . Pascal had covert plans to eventually lose Wolfie. They stood in a circle of people, all of whom Wolfie knew from the gym – and, while they eagerly whispered their narcotic testimonies and confessed to being loaded with drugs, not one showed the slightest sign of festive exuberance. Pascal danced on the spot, shaking his water bottle like a maraca. He scanned the room hopefully for other people he knew – or used to know. Suddenly, like an answered prayer, Tammy appeared. She was accompanied by a gaggle of Goths and neo-primitives. The two opposing clusters sneered at each other, like warring tribes; clearly no one's drugs had kicked in enough to override the vast differences in their aesthetic and political leanings. As Pascal began to chat with Tammy, Wolfgang and his acquaintances gradually moved a safer distance away.

'They all look like they've got carrots up their arses, she whispered to Pascal.

'Darling, they'd need watermelons before they'd feel a thing.'

'Well, if they're having a good time now, I'd hate to see 'em when they're miserable.'

Pascal suddenly felt a rush of something. He'd missed Tammy terribly and went to hug her. She was a touch cool at first but eventually responded with equal affection.

'So that's it, is it Tam? I don't see you any more?'

'Well, I hardly thought you'd want to after . . .' she looked down at her cigarette which was poised in an elaborate wire holder, à la *Sunset Boulevard,* 'well, you know.'

'It's no fun being banished, Tam.'

'That really wasn't my intention.' She lightened up and turned momentarily into Norma Desmond, taking an elaborate drag from the cigarette. 'But wha' do I care about friends? I've got an oil well, pumping, pumping, pumping.'

Pascal glanced gloomily over at Wolfie, 'I wish I had something pumping. Fancy a dance?'

Tam looked toward her entourage, which seemed to be edging onto the floor. A savage-looking dyke with a spiked collar was toying with her girlfriend's nipple ring, while a crusty boy on a leash circled them in a most peculiar piece of choreography. 'The boy's deaf,' she said, by way of an explanation. 'Totally wild sex, I'm told, and judging by the sounds I've heard from his room I wouldn't be the least bit surprised. Did I tell you I saw "the other" before?'

'The other?' queried Pascal.

'Humphrey, Dill Brain.'

'Oh.' Pascal feigned disinterest while acknowledging privately that he would spend the rest of his night with eyes peeled. 'How is the dear?'

'Fine. He was with some gorgeous black guy and an excruciatingly beautiful American girl who seemed to be on another planet altogether. You know Humphrey, he collects them like seashells on a beach. He's put on a few kilos, I managed to notice, and I'm not usually the sort who does. He was wearing some expensive shirt-thing that tried to disguise it. He looks good, though. How is it everyone I know who's HIV-positive seems to be getting fatter these days?'

'The drugs – steroids to stop the wasting, I expect.' Pascal danced around Tammy and noticed from the corner of his eye that Wolfie and his gang were moving further away. Soon the crowd would swallow them; they'd be lost to view. Then Pascal could say it was Wolfgang who had wandered off.

'Well I can guarantee the drugs he's on tonight won't be contributing to any further weight gain.'

Pascal threw his hands in the air. Something nice was happening to him. The Faithless song that boomed darkly in the hall was about making wild love on the heath, *tearing off tights with my teeth.* He loved that song – even if he never got to do any of those wild, animal things these days.

'I don't think any of us will be gaining fat tonight. I'll be thin as an angel come Monday.'

'And suffering the mean reds come Tuesday,' Tammy added.

'Depends how long I keep going. I've got the whole of next week off.'

'People aren't supposed to take party drugs with all that combination crap are they?'

Pascal laughed. 'You're not supposed to smoke while you're pregnant, or mix alcohol with sedatives, or drink and drive, or eat apples without washing them. We are talking about Humphrey, remember.'

Blaise was relaxing a little. He remembered Teresa flaunting that elaborate cigarette holder, so Elliot must have seen her later on in the night but Blaise never so much as glimpsed Elliot that time. It was very easy not to see people in a crowd of 25,000, though funnily enough Pascal usually managed to bump into the few individuals he was studiously avoiding at least three or four times in the course of one of those parties.

He couldn't remember doing anything that particular Mardi Gras which could feasibly come back to haunt him. He hadn't danced with Teresa that night, nor had they tackled any of those raw issues about their friendship. They'd only had the briefest chat because Blaise was still with Woodie, who had been brooding and difficult at first. Blaise had wished in vain that he would find Teresa after he'd lost Woodie. As it was, he'd wandered around on his own most of the time. Woodie had said he would be in the Dome, but he'd walked around it twice and still not seen his lover.

Pascal's explicit problem when he was under the influence was that if he was looking for someone in particular, half the people in the crowd tended to take on the appearance of the one he sought. Woodie never seemed to be at the appointed meeting place during their pre-arranged times, but then who ever was? At least he knew Woodie was on reasonably good drugs, and unlikely to be moping drunk somewhere in a maudlin torpor.

Woodie refused to believe he had a drinking problem – alcoholics often did. Pascal had read this in one of those books written for the partners of alcoholics that he'd secretly procured. The trouble with Woodie was that he was aware enough of the problem to hardly drink at all. When he did, it was almost always a protest. He was like those women in Imperial China who consumed opium in levels directly proportionate to their degree of marital discontent. Blaise could go to one of Woodie's work dinners and he wouldn't touch a drop – he'd drink Diet Coke all night. But when it was something of Blaise's, he'd knock back the alcoholic drinks fast. It was as if he was warning Blaise in no uncertain terms that they had better not stay long or they'd have another launch scenario on their hands. The next day, when Blaise complained about the mess his lover had gotten into, he'd be furious: 'I hardly ever drink, not like you! You get plastered a couple of times a week.' And Blaise couldn't say much because, in a way, it was true. Booze, Blues.

XVII

Woodrow's eyes were burning with fatigue. Not many pages to go, so he may as well get it over with. A security guard came by and Woodie pretended to be working. It was after seven on a Friday night. He'd never before shown such dedication to his job, but the guard recognised him and meandered on. Woodie wondered if there wasn't something in the guard's eye that hinted at a porn scenario but he recognised this fantasy as a by-product of reading Elliot's prurient innuendo. He felt tainted by Elliot's book, it coaxed him into cultivating feelings – sleazy, evil inklings he'd always struggled to keep at bay.

. . . 'No one can ever entirely be there for you,' Wolfgang thought as he descended the stairs. He'd wandered off and not seen Pascal for some time, hours perhaps. Excitement and euphoria pulsed through him. Perhaps he was better off on his own, not watching out for Pascal all the time – steering him away from the scrapes and dangers that a lot of Pascal's old, less responsible friends would merrily lead him into. 'All those pretentious wankers who had some fucked-up notion he wasn't good enough for Pascal. And what was that about earlier? That look from Tammy, the vicious little space cake.' Still, it was not the time to feel ill-will towards people, not while on ecstasy, not on the night of nights.

He wouldn't have gone down there if Pascal hadn't wandered off with Tam and that freak brigade of hers, but they'd put a DJ in the toilets downstairs this year. Now that he had to see. As he rounded the corner and joined the Indian file of toilet-goers, his eyes met the gaze of an exiting parade of punters. It was like an eerie changeover, their whacked-out faces flawed and human in the harsh stairwell lighting. He stared into huge pupils, and huge pupils stared back. Then he heard it, the slinky acid jazz. A slowly flashing red light had created a carnal oven of fleshy tones. A meaty mix of maleness that even someone of Wolfie's moral fibre couldn't fail to be weakened by.

He only wanted a look, but it was a difficult environment to stand outside. It was a subjective place, not an objective one. It was impossible to just dance to the music, or to dance in any conventional way. The collective energy of the men, and the heated crowd absorbed in the serious business of pleasure, conspired to lure him in.

Sweat from the soaked torsos acted as a lubricant and he feared he was lost, for these were the ranks of terrible men he fought daily against joining. The monsters of the deep. The fallen ones. This was the party's nether world, and what went on down here had angered him in the past. It had tempted boyfriends, destroyed sacred intimacies. He gasped. His drugs had another wind in them, and he wondered what would happen if he sacrificed himself to the mercury of desire rising within him. What would become of him in this terrible slick sea of sexual anarchy?

His desire wouldn't subside, he was losing to it. The heat in his head was a nail-bomb. Soho in his skull. And the hardness in his shorts made him feel explosive. Perhaps he shouldn't have taken drugs if this was the power they wielded. He'd always vowed to not be like *that*. Boys like that appalled him. But now, almost against his will, someone stroked the swelling in his strained leather codpiece, stroked it and made to free its inhabitant with their hands. 'No!' he growled and moved along, but he wasn't escaping. He moved further, deeper into the crowd – and it wasn't a crowd you could just free yourself from. It was a crush. Once you'd penetrated it, it penetrated back. Someone else was at him now and there was no use protesting. When two, then four, then more hands touched him, he was lost; his head swam and beads of perspiration rolled down his face. But it was worse – or better – because soon he felt the wetness, the hotness of a mouth that threatened to steal his very spirit from the weeping snake's eye on which it sucked. 'Oh, God,' he moaned and fell against the cubicle door. The fight was over, a fledgling joy had replaced it. That in turn gave way to an unprecedented hunger and that, finally, to an uncontrollable, chemically crazed, bestial lust.

Time became extinct as a concept, and a hostile, homophobic world vanished as busy boys dared to invent their own corner of heaven. Wolfie cried out, as did others, and his senses eventually returned enough for him to involve himself in the pleasuring of his private, eager platoon (because that was how he saw it suddenly). And he looked down at the man who had spent so long working with his hungry mouth on the very hardest part of Wolfie.

His breath caught abruptly, but the pleasure was too intense to withdraw. It was Humphrey who stared up at him with elfin eyes and a vague, smug recognition. 'Fuck me!' muttered Wolfie. Humphrey stood up. 'First through a glass darkly, now face to face,' murmured his rival of old.

The action seemed to go on around them now – distorted muzak in a surreal elevator on its way to God knows where. There were frenzied pockets of action here, screamingly intense ones there. Wolfie could hear the struggle of others, perhaps a Faustian struggle similar to his own. Spectators and hecklers, all unwittingly caught up in the carnival, losing themselves to deeper and darker levels of entanglement. Men who had only come to play with their hands battled with themselves as they gave in to mouths. And those who had been prepared for simple, glorious oral gratification struggled against bolder, more shameful intrusions. It was as though some twinkling, mischievous sprite danced above them, flinging magical dust into the corners where activity waned or the carnal symphony had reached a low ebb.

'You better be careful, Wolfgang,' whispered Humphrey into the other's ear. 'Say "fuck me" loud enough in here and your wish could be their command.'

'Did you know it was me?' Wolfie sounded gruff.

'What difference does it make?'

It made a lot of difference, but for a moment even Wolfie couldn't see how it did. He kissed Humphrey, though he didn't know why – perhaps to shut him up – and then slid to his knees before him. He couldn't believe what he was doing but admitted to himself that curiosity played a part. Was he bigger? Yes, damn him.

Wolfie swallowed his pride, swallowed Pascal's pride and swallowed his own words as he swallowed his lover's ex-lover's cock.

'I must say,' Humphrey whispered, 'I can't believe you're doing this. I'm simply transfixed by the shock and implications of it.'

Wolfie stood. 'You're transfixed by the fucking pleasure and filth of it, you are! You must never tell Pascal, alright? There are some things . . . Well, you know?'

Humphrey raised an eyebrow in the gloomy pink light. 'There are some things . . . you can't bear to know about yourself, I think is what you're trying to say. "The bread of deceit is sweet to a man but later his mouth shall be filled with gravel." Now get back down there and finish what you started, and pray I don't have any kidney stones' . . .

Blaise screamed, with shock, with anger and with the sheer insanity of it all, then wept a little in a hopeless, miserable way. 'Stupid, idiotic, fucking Woodie. The one trap, the one and only time it truly mattered to Blaise that his lover *not* be unfaithful – he was. He'd rather Woodie had shagged his way through every bar and toilet in the city than engage in that one single tryst. No wonder Woodie had been so sheepish and such a lost boy when he finally found him again at that feted, fateful party. But nothing could ease this anger. He wasn't surprised at Elliot. Elliot had probably spent half the night down there, he wouldn't have known whose cock he was sucking half the time, nor would he have cared. Getting a mouthful of Woodie was like winning the lottery. A mouthful of cock and a novel full of plot.

Woodrow was frozen where he sat. He would never read the rest of the book. He'd read enough. What could be said in the last ten pages that would save him? He was suddenly Glenn Close in *Dangerous Liaisons*, wiping the powder from her nose. No longer a part of society, not fit to show his face.

Now he knew why Blaise had been behaving so oddly towards him. He must have already read the whole story. Still, it was fiction. He might still be able to convince Blaise that it never happened – or that, if it did, it was nothing like Elliot's description. He could say he brushed against him, that he'd gone down there with some friends just to check out the DJ, to heckle the sleaze-bags. He wondered if Blaise would ring Elliot. Would he believe Elliot's story over his own? Surely he'd hate Elliot too much now to ever speak to him again. What a loathsome coward Elliot Bernard truly was. How many lives did he want to wreck with his book? Some things should never be spoken about.

He would lose Blaise for sure now. He knew it without a doubt. He wouldn't mention any of what he'd read; Blaise could bring it up if he saw fit. Damage control would be the next step. Their affair had been about more things than just love. The important thing now was to look after himself. He needed to see Gavin – more than just see Gavin, he needed someone he could talk to. A soul mate. Elliot had got him all worked up with his literary filth and someone had to help sort out the mess in his head.

XVIII

Blaise took a drink from a new bottle of whisky, a bottle he'd hidden from you-know-who. The other bottle in the lounge was empty, Woodie had obviously taken Blaise's recent absences as an opportunity to polish it off and wallow in self-pity. The thought that Woodie could come home at any moment had him feeling very tense. He didn't know what to do with himself or where to go. With two Scotches down, however, it did occur to him he could try ringing Elliot, even if it was only to abuse him.

Blaise wasn't angry at Elliot for his part in the sexual encounter with Woodie. It was Elliot's nature to challenge and transgress every taboo. Somehow, transgressions of that nature were Elliot's purpose. It was as if he'd been placed on Earth merely to demonstrate the corruption and double standards we poor frail creatures are capable of perpetrating. No. His sin this time was in the telling. He recognised that his leaving Elliot all those years ago may have been more devastating for Elliot than he had let on at the time, but retaliation on this scale was too much! How many people would read this book? Certainly, everyone who knew Blaise would be reading it once word got out.

He picked up the phone . . .

'Hello.'

'It's me, Blaise.'

'Well, well, well. Howdy stranger,' came Teresa's reply. 'To what do I owe the pleasure of this call?'

'I don't know that I'd call it pleasure. I hate my life, it's a mess.'

'I take it you've read *Je Louse* then?'

'Yes.'

'I thought it was a hoot, though sometimes Elliot's self-obsession got a bit much for me. He rang me last night, isn't that spooky? I loved my "Tammy". I wonder what the people who weren't in it are doing tonight?'

'Who cares what they're doing? I'm jealous of them all. I hope the book flops majorly. Remember, I am "Pascal" – can you imagine how that makes me feel?'

'Better than Woodrow, I'll bet.'

'Fuck Woodrow. What did Elliot say?'

'Nothing much. What do you care anyway?'

'You're right, what do I care? Oh, Teresa. Can you believe that – what happened at the party?'

Teresa was eating something juicy on the other end of the line. 'Oh *that*, I already knew about *that*,' she slurped.

'Wha' d' ya mean?'

'You're talking about that revolting toilet scene, aren't you?'

'Of course.'

'Oh God, Blaise, we were with Elliot most of the night. He told us what he'd been up to and with whom. I wasn't the least bit surprised, I have to say.'

'And you never bothered to tell me?'

'We haven't exactly been close the last couple of years. To say Woodrow hadn't ingratiated himself to me would be a slight understatement, don't you think? What would it have looked like if I came to you with bitchy snatches of gossip? You wouldn't have believed it, you'd have hated me for telling you – and I bet Woodie would have denied it. Men like him always lie about things like that – believe me I know! . . . Blaise . . . Blaise, are you still there?'

'Yeah.'

'You're in shock, aren't you, babe?'

'So who else knew?'

'I don't know, everyone who was outside Dome with us when he returned from that filthy toilet block. He was gone for over an hour, so if it's any comfort to you I'm sure Woodie wasn't the only one who got to *meat* the author that night. He was quite dishevelled by the time he returned . . .'

'It's no comfort whatsoever. So you don't think the toilet thing will come as a surprise to any of our old tribe?'

'Um . . . in a word . . . noooo.'

'So I've been pretty much a laughing stock since that night?'

'Laughing stock is too strong, a casualty of irony would be a better appraisal. What are you going to do?'

'I'm leaving Woodrow. I'd decided that before I even got to *that* bit in the book. He's having an affair.'

'Surprise, surprise.'

'Don't be so sarcastic.'

Teresa let out an exhausted sigh. 'Well, what do you expect? I suppose you'll be wanting me back as a friend, then?'

The line was silent. Blaise could hear background TV noise in Teresa's lounge room – *but get in now because the offer is limited*. The disembodied voice struck Blaise as an omen.

'I guess I will.'

'What about the flat?'

'God, Teresa, you sound like my mum – every emotional decision has a material consequence. Who cares about the fucking flat or the shitting car?'

Teresa took another squelchy bite of her orange. 'I can guarantee there's someone else who won't be quite so cavalier about such matters.'

'You're a fucking witch, you know that – and quite frankly, my dear, the way I feel about things right now he could have the lot just so I could be rid of him.'

'Yes, well, you'll change your mind about that in due course. Mark my words.'

'Yes, Mum.'

Gavin seemed different when Woodie explained to him how his relationship was falling apart because of Elliot Bernard. Suddenly there was a distance between them, and the situation was difficult to explain unless you knew all the parties – and had read the book.

'Woodie, this thing between you and me has never been about all that serious emotional crap. You get what I mean. This was, like, extracurricular. Fucking for fuck's sake, which has been really excellent, but you know I've got Rory. And you and I have never been into talking about deep stuff – man, we're gym buddies, skin friends. Fun and muscles, so I don't know I can really help you out here. Also, Rory's back tonight and it's getting late. I said to you, only come over before seven.'

'I thought Rory was cool about everything.'

'Well there's cool, Woodie, and then there's having your nose rubbed in stuff, if you dig. I wouldn't do that to him.'

'I'd better go then,' said Woodie. He was shattered, and the nose-rubbing reference hadn't improved his state of mental health. He'd thought they really did have something going – a connection – but a mask had descended over Gavin's face.

He wanted to cry. He even wanted Blaise back again, but as he'd made Blaise play by his rules the last few years what hope was there? It was all fucking Elliot's fault – motor mouth, pretentious cunt Elliot and his epic wankathons that are supposed to pass for literature.

XIX

Clouds had been gathering all evening. It had been looking like it was going to bucket down hours ago but it hadn't. Instead the sky had thickened to molasses, creating an unearthly, weighty stillness.

Blaise devoured a tube of Pringles. Even with all the clouds and depression, once he'd popped, he couldn't stop. Cars rushed along New South Head Road and he watched from the window, wondering which might contain Woodie, and hoping none of them did. Perhaps Woodie was having sex with Gavin. A repulsive thought, decided Blaise. Perhaps he'd had an accident. He paused for a moment, thinking how convenient and respectable widowhood could be. He felt like Joan Crawford in *Mildred Pierce* or Barbara Stanwyck in *Double Indemnity*. 'The insurance would just about pay off the mortgage, too,' he thought, then immediately paid for this evil notion as a sickening bolt of guilt struck him.

Blaise was floating three floors above the world – in between lives, it seemed. In neighbouring apartments he could see proper, living people going about their business: cooking, laughing, drinking wine, glued to the TV and dressing – mmmm, dressing. He peered out as a guy in briefs searched for something in a stack of boxes. 'He must be the new one.' He went to pour some more Scotch. He required a beverage that could cut through the fat from the chips. 'I don't need anyone. I can sit myself here, listen to CDs, eat chips until I'm as fat as a Christmas pig and drink whisky until Jesus comes back and the whole planet can go to buggery.'

No sooner had he said it than a terrible booming hullabaloo startled him back into a more conventional frame of awareness. It was as if an aeroplane were about to crash through the roof; he prepared to assume the 'brace' position. At once, it was upon him, a thundering sound unlike anything he'd ever heard. Then the glass. First one of the west-facing windows shattered, then another, as if someone were firing a gun through them – a terrible homophobic siege. Smash, clang, patinck. All he could hear was glass breaking and the din of a thousand car alarms in an apocalyptic cacophony. 'What?' he screamed to no one in particular. He noticed a cricket-ball-sized hailstone on the lounge-room floor, then another and another. There was hardly any glass left in the windows, just pernicious dangling shards and an apartment yawning open to the invading elements. Dozens of the icy monsters were piling up on the carpet. He tried to move the TV and stereo, but they were too close to the window. He would be killed if one of those fuckers hit him.

Above him was the other sound. Sturdy terracotta roof tiles, breaking like bone china; the lumps of ice coming through the plaster ceiling – four, five, six of them. 'Oh, God!' He could smell electrical smoke from the back of the amplifier.

The hail no sooner subsided than the rain took over. He was running around like a lunatic. What must he have looked like to the neighbours? 'Fuse box, fuse box . . .' he couldn't remember where it was. Woodie would know, Elliot would know. 'Oh, Woodie!' Had Blaise conjured this up – was it all his fault? Was Woodrow in the car, involved in some terrible accident?

As soon as the thought escaped him, he heard the sirens. It was a disaster, surely thousands would be dead. It sounded as if every emergency vehicle in the city was out in all this bedlam, conjured up by the black heart of a jealous, angry queen.

Chaos had reached the street below, while Blaise busily dragged out every bucket and saucepan he could find to catch the indiscriminate torrents of water now pouring through the ceiling in three separate rooms. He unplugged the electricals, wiped them down and reached for the phone. At least that was working, he dialled 0414 . . . 'Hiya, this is Woodie, can't talk, you know what to do.'

'Woodrow, it's Blaise.' He realised he was sobbing roughly as he spoke. He hadn't figured he was in such a state, and regretted it as the silent voicemail awaited his speech: 'Everything's fucked, ruined. I don't know what to do. Call me ASAP.' He hung up the phone, then thought about what he'd said. Had he been talking about the hailstorm or their lives together? He sniffled. 'Whatever.'

Woodie was heading for home. Not because he wanted to, but because he had nowhere else to go. He'd heard the long, strangely unbroken clap of thunder heralding the approaching storm and had found himself on the elevated section of road that bypasses Bondi Junction when lethal rocks of sorbet started flying. All the cars had stopped in their tracks. It was like driving on marbles. Even Woodie had let out an un-macho squealing lament when the reinforced windscreen shattered like brittle toffee. Once splintered, rocks began coming through. He'd crawled into the back seat, only to hear the rear window go as well. The thunderous pummelling on the roof echoed his deepest remorse and torment.

Cars were beginning to honk, a few dazed drivers wandered around their wreckages while a police car cruising by with a megaphone warned drivers to 'REMAIN

INSIDE YOUR VEHICLES.' The woman in the car next to Woodie was crying. He felt a sudden desire to go and comfort her but realised he had tears streaming down his own face. He couldn't have her see those. And then the phone was ringing in the boot, where his briefcase was. There was ice everywhere, inches of ice in a city that never sees snow. He rocked himself gently in the back seat until the honking became too loud. He climbed back into the front and drove at ten kilometres per hour. Watching the world through a savage, bullet-sized hole. A heavenly bullseye.

XX

Elliot Bernard sat in front of the TV in his sublet, two-room East Village apartment. It was quite a comedown after the Long Island extravaganza, which Lex and he had been house-sitting for the last eighteen months. Dario and Constantina Villiers de l'Isle had returned from Dario's secondment at the Sorbonne and were understandably keen to summer in the glorious home they'd missed so terribly.

'The French were aloof, the Italians divine but guarded, and the Germans were all workaholics. Dario's more utilitarian in his cultural intercourse, aren't you, darling – he swears that America leads the world in plumbing.' Constantina had been all gush on her return and Elliot had preferred to return to the relative silence of Downtown Manhattan.

On the sort of travel budget Dario and Constantina commanded, Elliot was amazed they should have been subjected to bad plumbing anywhere. He wondered quietly how people amassed wealth such as theirs. Lex had theories and gossip about it – but Elliot usually forgot apocryphal anecdotes as soon as they were uttered – an unfortunate failing in a writer, perhaps, but it saved him from lawyers and their bills. Well, so far it had.

The fortune must surely have been inherited, or maybe Constantina's art dealership was a multi-million-dollar business. Whatever the case, academia certainly wouldn't support their lifestyle and maintaining a house such as theirs in the Hamptons seemed an enormous waste, given they were seldom in it for more than three months of the year.

Still, it was better living there for the winter than in a boarded-up Fire Island beach house, as Elliot had done his first year in New York. He'd nearly gone mad: he'd seen ghosts, almost died in a blizzard and got so lonely he could have screamed. That winter would prove to be his one and only foray into the monastic life. The sexual dangers of the summer were a tea dance compared to the winter perils. Scott of the Antarctic, everyone had called him whenever he'd returned to Manhattan for medication, supplies and a life-affirming sexual encounter.

Lex had just enjoyed his first major off-Broadway success, with a play entitled *Meat for the Morrow Man*, but had become romantically entangled with the gorgeous Hispanic star, José Cortez. José had turned out to be a 'bunny boiler' – a term coined from the movie *Fatal Attraction* for people with psychotically possessive natures who were likely to boil family pets if amorous matters didn't go entirely their way.

All drama aside, it was beginning to look like the apartment was not big enough for two writers and their fluctuating fortunes and egos. Lex had stayed on Long Island and was about to move into some loft in the Village. It seemed their love affair was ending. If Elliot was honest with himself, he'd admit he was never really *in* love with Lex. He was sexy, for sure – and Elliot could always enjoy that part of the arrangement – but Lex was so distracted, so ambitious and eight years younger. Elliot had always thought eight years wouldn't make a difference, but these days he found it could. Elliot needed someone more his own speed.

Je Louse was selling satisfactorily but his UCLA contract had finished. He thanked God for that. One more of those flights to LA, one more rent-a-car and he would have had a breakdown. The job at Princeton – a few guest lectures – hadn't turned into anything more substantial, so he'd found himself pining for Sydney again. So much so that he'd been looking at real estate on the net and making definite plans. With all that rent-free living out on Long Island, he'd saved a lot of money and the Australian dollar was very low at present. He could do very well if he went back now. And he longed to own another Sydney apartment. A home of his own. In the meantime, he'd just have to go back and rent. He had decided that, at thirty-nine, he was too old for couches and house-sitting. He'd roamed long enough, and far enough. He knew you could only ever really belong to one place and somewhere along the line he had to decide which place that would be.

Elliot should really have been working on an article for the *Advocate*, which was already overdue, but instead he watched one of the myriad boy bands performing on TV. He'd lost track of their names, he couldn't keep up, but they were always new and usually pleasant to watch. This particular outfit was singing some insufferably soft-cock romantic song which, these days, seemed capable of milking the pocket money from the kiddies. The boys meted out some clichéd piece of choreography on the girders of the Brooklyn Bridge, and it occurred to him that their talents might be better employed in the making of pornographic movies. He smiled, thinking their careers couldn't possibly be any more ephemeral in that industry than in the music game.

He thought about going and getting one of those tantric lingam massages from a gorgeous black masseur around the corner, but he was too gripped by ennui. Besides, so far those massages had failed to be 'tantric' in any way for Elliot. 'Man, you need to move away from this mortal ejaculation shit, you can't drain your soul but your spirit gets weaker every time you mess on my table.' No, Elliot wouldn't go again. He was too ashamed after that lecture. Elliot's spirit had 'leaked' far too much in one lifetime to try putting a cork in it now.

Perhaps he could ring Blaise. He'd been putting it off. His heart skipped a beat every time he thought about what his reaction might have been to the book. That story had been a huge gamble. Huge. But it may have worked. Instead, he decided on something a little safer:

'Hello.'

'Teresa, Elliot.'

'Well, aren't you just the world's greatest shit-stirrer and coward?'

'Coward?'

'Well you couldn't *really* be any further away, could you? And that book, Elliot, you're just too wicked – you know that?'

'Well, it's the truth isn't it?'

'Truth, shmooth. You're a home-wrecker, you are.'

'What sort of home, though?'

'I didn't say I disapproved, did I? That party scene couldn't have happened to a more deserving chap than Woof Woof Woodrow.'

'Have you seen Blaise?'

'Nup, never do hardly, "he's on such a short leash I can't even see the chain any more".'

'Alright Terri, you can play Tammy when the film rights sell.'

'I already know my lines off by heart.'

'Do you think Blaise will be angry?'

'You didn't ring to talk to me, did you? You just want to find out about Blaise. Blaise, Blaise, Blaise. If I didn't know better, Mr Long Island ISD, I'd say you were still in lurrrve with that lily-livered scoundrel. Surely you, our great white international hope, isn't longing for the failed law student. He still works at the same job, I know that much.'

'Who said anything about love? Terri, surely you realise I'm far too damaged now to be entrapped by something so sweet and banal as love?'

'So Humphrey said in the book. Then what's happened to the playwright, the bloodhound and the Keith Haring?'

'Well, the Haring was never ours. It belongs to the Villiers de l'Isles of Long Island. Lex has Glasnost in his new Greenwich Village apartment for security. He is also on a very short leash and I'm all on my lonesome in the East Village sublet that I've got a week to vacate.'

'Where will you go then?'

'Home.'

'No?'

'Yes, flat 6/189A Elizabeth Bay Road to be precise – you know, those serviced joints?'

Teresa screamed. 'I don't believe it. No one ever comes back from New York – alive.'

'I know, I know, Lee Tulloch and all the other expats will just have to do without me, I'm afraid. Let's hope one of the unis will have me back.'

'Elliot, this is Australia; you'd only have had to take a ride to the top of the Empire State Building and you'd have an internationally recognised doctorate in altitudinal semiotics. When do you leave?'

'Next Wednesday.'

'Email me the flight details and I'll pick you up.'

'You're a doll. Don't tell the *other*, will you.'

'I'll do exactly as I see fit, you arsehole. Now fuck off.'

'Next week then?'

'I'll be there, don't you worry.'

XXI

. . . Humphrey hunted through his reference books, in an eager bid to find greater minds and nobler words with which to express the feelings he'd tried to gather in his heart and capture in the hand-stitched safety net of fiction. The greats were all there, and they were all dead. A catechism of conflicting platitudes. He found a Blaise Pascal quote: *The last act is bloody, however charming the rest of the play may be.* He wished he'd found it in time to put it at the front of the novel.

So many fools and so much folly. He was a fatalist, though. He knew that in the play of life, we'd all been cast in our respective roles long before the auditions began. He loathed his role as much as he rejoiced in it. He, too, was an historical inevitability. It is often said that life's finest artists – not the bullshit artists, the self-aggrandisement artists or the status artists but the real-life success artists – are those who know when to tell the truth and when to leave truth to tell itself. There are books full of philosophical quotes labouring the virtues of truth, listing testimonies to its all-pervading power or its eternal elusiveness. Truth exists in eternal conflict, however, and can be worse than lies. White lies and black truths. As William Blake wrote: 'A truth that's told with bad intent, Beats all the lies you can invent.'

Humphrey contemplated his many possible motivations. The wounded Humphrey, who had been left for another man. The defeated Humphrey, tail between his legs, who had wanted to have his cake and eat it too. Humphrey the egomaniac, who could take his pick of boys as long as money was in his pockets and success was in his stars.

Humphrey was all these sorry souls yet none of them at all. He was first and foremost a lover, and he chose Thomas Jefferson's 'Letter to Henry Lee' to justly express his feelings at having written such an exposé: 'There is not a truth existing which I fear, or would wish unknown to the whole world'. And Humphrey hoped that Pascal would know the truth about truth, that it invariably came by way of a limping messenger. A wounded man with a heart on his sleeve, too shy to ever knock on Pascal's door.

'Oh, my God!' shouted Blaise to the blue sky he could glimpse through his ceiling. The whole book was a love letter, written as only a love letter could be by one Elliot

Bernard. 'Could it really be meant for me?' – or was this ending an expedient way of calming Blaise down, some romantic literary Phenergan for his long-lost baby love.

Blaise dropped the finished tome by his chair. He'd taken a week off work to look for somewhere else to live and to wait for the emergency services to put a tarpaulin over their ravaged roof. It was five o'clock now, and he'd given up on them materialising for yet another day. The storm had been, after all, the most expensive natural disaster the country had ever seen. When it was couched in those terms Blaise felt he should be suffering even more, but decided he'd suffered quite enough.

If it rained again, that would mean another sleepless night of emptying buckets to protect the two floors of residents below. Woodie could be on duty tonight. Blaise was over it. The flat would have to be fixed before it could be sold, and he knew Woodie would take his time to get that process into motion. Fortunately theirs was only a one-bedroom flat and Blaise had said he couldn't afford to pay rent and mortgage. He'd hoped that it would be Woodie who'd move out, but Woodie had been incredulous at the accusations made in the book. Quite resistant to blame.

'It's fiction, Blaise, it's a fucking Elliot fantasy. Sure I went in there to check out the DJ. Yes, I saw Elliot down there. End of story. You think I'd really let that trough-pig suck my dick?'

Blaise was unmoved: 'Matthew fucked Mark fucked Luke fucked John, who lay on the bed that I lie on . . .'

'What are you on about now? If you want to take his fictitious word over mine you go right ahead, but I'm not having my life turned upside down because you can't tell truth from fantasy. Move out if you can't stand it here!'

Blaise never wanted to feel his current levels of anger towards anyone, much less his lover. He feared it was something approaching hatred. He thought about Elliot sitting on that couch in the Hamptons or wherever. 'Nice work if you can get it,' he sighed, wondering if the tarps would ever arrive. He couldn't be bothered with looking at flats in the paper. He could hardly be bothered with anything at all. He was simply relieved that Woodie was at work, taking with him the awful brooding angst that permeated their broken home. He decided he'd ring Teresa; perhaps he could have a drink with her. She certainly wouldn't come around when 'the other' was at home.

XXII

'Teresa speaking.'

'It's Blaise. So you're at home today, then?'

'I just got in.'

'Can we go out for a drink tonight? The flat's depressing me.'

There was a pause on the phone. Blaise wondered if he was being too presumptuous about the resumption of friendship. 'Sorry, Terri, I know it's short notice. We can go another time.'

'It's OK, it's just I'm, aahhh, going to some house-warming drinks with an old friend in Elizabeth Bay. You can come too, if you're up to it.'

'Anyone I know?'

'I'm sure you'd have met him, but years ago.'

'I don't know whether I'm up to new people right now.'

'There's nothing new about this one. You'd like him, he's been around, this guy.'

'What the hell, should I get a bottle?'

'Yeah, I'll come by in twenty and pick you up.'

This was what Blaise needed. Something to get him away from the flat and the terminal illness of this relationship.

Teresa's car honked, and Blaise ran downstairs. Since the hailstorm, her old 1968 Merc's bodywork looked like a lunar landscape, and she had no insurance to fix it.

'It's worthless,' she said. 'It can't be fixed and it can't be sold. I'll have to drive this car for the rest of my bloody life.' She dropped it into gear.

'So who did you say this guy is?'

'I didn't.' She was smiling as she ashed her fag out the window. A flurry of sparks blew back in. *Do You Know the Way to San José* was on the radio.

'What the fuck station have you got the radio on? I hate this song.'

'*Throw a hundred down and buy a car*,' sang Teresa, even after he'd changed the channel.

'God, have you started listening to hits and memory stations since you stopped being my friend? Good job I rang you when I did.' She'd started singing another song.

'*Iiiin my mind there's a place, on my lips there's a name . . .*'

'I know, *from New York to LA . . .*'

'Ay ayayayayay ooh *from New York to LA* oooh hoo hoo who?'

'Is this person someone from America? It's not a friend of Elliot's, is it?'

'Nagh. This guy makes our old Elliot look like a nun.'

They pulled up outside a block of serviced apartments.

'Oh God, Terri.' They were climbing the front steps. 'This is where bloody Elliot used to stay when he was over. I had to sneak in here to see him one time.'

They rang the doorbell.

'Well if it's all over with what's-his-face, then you need sneak no more.'

She'd no sooner finished speaking than the door opened and Elliot was in front of them.

'Fuck.'

'Fuck.'

And, in unison, 'Teresa, you bitch!'

Blaise went to move back, but Teresa had her arm around him, blocking his escape. She was pushing him over the threshold. Blaise was thinking two things: fight or flight? But Blaise's pride had always been an easily suppressed component of his splendid being, and the bottles of champagne at this terrible moment in his life were an irresistible temptation.

'Did she trick you here?' asked Elliot. His usual confidence had gone into a very humble hibernation.

'Yes, she did.' He looked angrily at Teresa, who seemed suddenly very interested in her fingernails.

'I'm not sure I'm ready to see you yet, Elliot. I'm still *dealing* with the book.'

Teresa looked up. 'Well, as you're here and I'm not driving you home – if you can call it that – we may as well have a drink to hailstorms and has-beens.'

The bewildered trio walked into the lounge. Elliot grabbed some glasses. Blaise sat down in an ugly, pastel-coloured leather armchair and formed himself into a knot of impossibly negative body language while looking at the flickering images on the TV screen. No one said a word for quite some time.

'Well ... isn't this fun?' said Teresa. 'Dear friends together at last, in front of the *telly*, just like the old days after a dance party ... Oops, did I say dance party?'

'Shut up, Teresa. It's not the *dance party* I care about.' Blaise skolled his champers and poured another.

'What is it you *do* care about?' asked Elliot, doing the same thing with his glass, as if they were playing a drinking game.

'Christ, Elliot! What do you think I care about? The unsafe sex, the betrayal of our intimacies, the portrayal of me as some spineless victim who's never been able to take control of my life or my desires ...' Suddenly the other two were staring at Blaise with curious expressions of disbelief pinned to their faces. Teresa let out a howl of laughter.

'Just because I never *have*, doesn't mean you have to

gloat about it in front of half the fucking world.'

'Blaise, you flatter me too much if you think half the world would ever read my books. There are about twenty people on the planet who would read Pascal as you. It's a work of fiction . . . It's a work of . . . love.' Elliot looked away, embarrassed. Blaise looked away, too, and Teresa didn't know where to look.

'IT'S NO USE TO ME!' shouted Blaise. He skolled another drink. Teresa poured herself one more and the game went on. 'And I have *no* intention of flattering you, for Christ's sake. What do I care how many people read it? My life's so fucking boring and awful that I can hardly stand living it at the moment – how can you expect people to pay money to read about it? Elliot, you've made my life a misery, and what the fuck are you doing here anyway? Haven't you got a dog to feed and a Lex to shag and lectures to do at Berkeley or NYU or somewhere?'

Blaise could feel the alcohol fuelling his passions.

'I'm back here now for good'.

'Hah. Whose good I wonder?' Blaise slammed his glass onto the glass table with a nasty crack. He jumped – he'd had enough of shattered glass for one week, but thankfully it hadn't broken.

'Lex got tempted away by a sultry young sociopath whom I'm old enough to have sired myself; Princeton was nearly impossible to get to from the Hamptons, so I spent half my time in the Manhattan apartment anyway; and Glasnost can't be shifted around the world without spending months in quarantine, he's far too temperamental for that.'

'What about the Keith Haring?' Blaise asked, his temper subsiding a little.

'That's exactly what I said.' Teresa was enjoying this.

'That wasn't ours.'

'That belonged to Countess Consuela Cunnilingus or something, didn't it, Elliot?' Teresa was swanning towards the kitchen in a manner befitting a leading New York socialite. 'I'm going to the *bathroom*, boys, for a crap.'

Elliot laughed. 'Sorry, darling, your accent was Queens not Manhattan.'

The two men sat at opposing ends of the smoked-glass coffee table.

'So . . .' said Elliot.

'Are you still off the fags?' enquired Blaise.

'The nicotine variety, yes.'

'Ha ha.'

'You can't smoke anywhere now anyway. New York's the worst. Americans are extraordinary like that. They'll virtually annihilate some third world country's environment for their own economic advancement, but threaten them with a few wisps of passive smoke and they'll drag you through every law-court and talk-show in the land.' Elliot was waffling nervously. 'You still off them?'

'Yes, but I've been thinking of taking them up again since I read the book. They might help my weight too, now I'm becoming *loose*. I suppose you'll be expecting an *Evita*-scale welcome?'

'I really just want some peace. A *Telegraph* journo's already been hounding my agent about my involvement with some Filipino mentorship scheme of dubious legality. I know nothing about it.'

'You always did have your finger in too many pies, didn't you, Elliot?' Blaise smiled with whimsical satisfaction.

'Perhaps, but I've never even been to the Philippines. So what's happening with you and Woodrow?'

'Don't ask, it's a horror story – and that's just the apartment chapter. As for . . . well, I can't talk to *you* about it. He wanted to sue you over the book. At least he did before he got to the party bit – which of course he denies profusely, but it's written all over his face. I feel like Hillary Clinton. Elliot, you really are a sleazy old dog, you know that? I told him you can't sue people for telling the truth.'

'Nonsense, they do it in the States all the time. Do you really think I'm wrong to have told that story?'

Blaise exhaled heavily and pressed the cool champagne flute against his flushed cheek.

'You think you have some inalienable right to prove that everyone else is tarred with the same brush as you.

Not everyone is a filth-monger, Elliot, and very few can hold a candle to you. I could really have done without it, you know.'

'All I wanted to do was show how absurd some of the double standards we live under are.'

'Sir, you are too noble! Well, thanks a million for allowing me to be the vehicle by which such absurdity could be illustrated. You were retaliating against me for leaving you – I realise that much.' Blaise paused and glanced out the window at the sun's fading rays. 'When we separated, you were so good about it and Woodrow was so ghastly. I never stood up for you. I feel awful about that. I'm weak, I know. But to use all your fame and power to crush us like that ... You'll never know how that makes *ordinary* folk like me feel.'

Blaise looked at Elliot, who wore an open, apologetic expression. Their eyes met, and Blaise felt a frightening explosion of desire deep inside himself. He could feel his face redden with it, and knew his weakness hadn't diminished with the years. He tried to change the subject but he could tell that Elliot had seen it, felt it. He'd read somewhere that the spoken word only ever accounted for thirty-five per cent of what was communicated in a conversation.

'Where's Teresa? She must have constipation or something.' Blaise turned away from Elliot towards the door.

Suddenly she appeared, with fresh lipstick applied.

'Oh, my God, is that the time? I have to meet this policy researcher for a drink. I met her in Canberra last week and I swear she's a dyke; they're so disingenuous, those political types. I want to introduce her to Carla who lives in our house.' Teresa was fussing in front of the mirror, wrestling with some chunky earrings. 'Sorry guys, I'm going to have to love and leave you.'

Blaise felt a wave of anger at Teresa for setting him up and then deserting.

After the first drink he'd been able to say to himself 'NO, you can never, *ever* go back.' After the second, he could still summon up enough anger to keep Elliot at arm's length, but after the third drink and in the absence of Terri, he didn't know what would become of him.

NO, that wasn't the problem. He knew exactly what would become of him. He could already see the lurid pornographic pinks of it in his mind's eye. Elliot was kissing Terri, showing her to the door. His mind went into fibrillation. Blaise was right where she wanted him. *Pavlov's dog: beg for Humphrey, jump for Humphrey, sit on Humphrey's bone*. The most Blaise could do was niggle a while longer. Fight the good fight. But even as he watched Elliot's endearingly familiar form make for the kitchen, and doubtless another bottle, he could see the future. All of it in wide-screen Imax.

Tonight: a ferocious rekindling of an interrupted passion – the mere thought of it made him weak. From there, Blaise would make protests about his independence, his need for space and Elliot would indulge him. It would all happen faster than these things should, but Blaise didn't mind because he was a marsupial, a cuddly little fella who could cope with the wildness of the forest as long as he had a pouch, a warm nest and a mate. Elliot might be the moral outback, the Uluru adventure, the Australian experience – but Blaise was the souvenir, the soft toy to keep by your pillow and warm your heart. He didn't fear anything anymore. He'd already faced the worst, and if there was trouble ahead, infidelities, God knows what all, he was old enough and ugly enough to cope. *Je Louse* had been a rare, savage, vulgar and rather corny love song. No one in history had been serenaded in such a way. Few would probably want to be.

He watched the froth rise to the top of the glass as Elliot poured. He remembered the fortune teller, 'best go with the American one though 'e's strange an' all'. Elliot shouldn't be drinking champagne if he was still on some of those pills – it would upset his stomach, all that acid. Still, that wasn't Blaise's concern just yet. 'Strange' is right, he thought, as he kicked off his shoes and unfolded his body a little – and what was all that about buzzards, anyway?

'Do you think you'll ever forgive me?' begged Elliot coyly, as he sat himself on the couch.

'Well, that all depends.' Blaise watched the bubbles

rising, tiny ones. This was expensive French duty-free stuff, fresh from the airport. Blaise knew there was plenty more where that came from. Cars and planes, Elliot and chains. The resumption of some adventurous hostilities with generous helpings of glorious byronic *amore* in Sydney's inexplicably surreal environment. The picture had never looked more attractive.

'Depends on what?'

Blaise felt his soul vibrate. 'On whether or not, in the heat of one long autumn night, you can make me forget the past and obscure the future.'

Elliot smiled. 'I can't tell you how glad I am to hear that. I can but try. I've gambled all my life but I think if I play my cards right, I might still hit the jackpot.'

Gridiron

It costs me never a stab nor squirm
To tread by chance upon a worm.
'Aha, my little dear,' I say,
'Your clan will pay me back one day.'

THOUGHT FOR A SUNSHINY MORNING,
Dorothy Parker

A clot of regret passed through Rose Elliot's heart as she contemplated the buffet table in the dining room. She wished she hadn't bothered to bring the sausage rolls and sponge cake that remained untouched at its centre. Blaise had said not to go to any trouble; he said he'd organised caterers, so there'd be nothing at all to do. Still, she'd wanted to do something. She hadn't wanted to arrive empty-handed. Even for this.

As it was, people were eating sushi, oysters – and all sorts of carefully prepared canapés she couldn't have put a name to. She was embarrassed now by her conspicuous plates of home-made fare. Berni loved sponge cakes, she remembered. She used to make two or three a week, and he would have gobbled down a whole one after school if she'd let him. Her head bobbed gently with the memory.

Spoiled his tea he would have, always had a sweet tooth, did Berni. There were no dishes to be done either. A dishwasher hummed away busily in the kitchen while two attractive youngsters in crisp white aprons and monogrammed catering uniforms attended to everything else.

Rose clutched her best handbag in her lap and she was still gripping a clump of tissues in her tiny liver-spotted fist. She stuffed the white bundle into the sleeve of her blue cardigan – the one she usually wore to church – with mother-of-pearl buttons and a Scotch thistle brooch that permanently adorned it. She couldn't decide whether she was hot or cold, and her frock crackled with static as it shifted against the nylon slip beneath it. People smiled at her as they passed – like they always do at gentle, white-haired ladies wearing pale-pink lipstick and spectacles. They especially did today, with a practised, difficult smile kept hidden in heart-shaped lockets for drizzly days. Rose's plump feet wriggled out of her good navy shoes, reviving pleasantly with the cool of the air. She never usually wore them for more than a couple of hours on Sundays.

She had been sitting like that since they returned from the chapel, if you could call *that* place a chapel. *All that talk about the spirit's journey and Berni's gift for shining light onto darkness. The celebrant – a celebrant at a funeral, would you believe – didn't look like a man of God to her and made scant mention of the Lord. He'd worn an earring, too.*

'Whosoever gather in My name, said the Lord. Well, we are all the whosoever, regardless of what others might think,' he'd cried from the pulpit. According to the celebrant, it was Elliot's struggle against the church, its dogma and double standards, that brought him so much closer to God. 'Some of us see no opposition, no conflict of interest between the differing types of love – and our expressions of these will not be tempered by religious nor societal convention. If it's love, the Lord won't mind! Life is a banquet and most poor suckers are starving to death. Not Berni. Who amongst us today could say Elliot Bernard ever acted without love?'

He'd certainly thrown down the gauntlet there, she'd thought, but there had not been one murmur of dissent.

'Elliot had the most extraordinary acceptance of his own death. Cheerfully he commanded Blaise, Teresa and myself to bring books to the hospital, in order that he might find the perfect quotes for his own eulogy or to be used in his forthcoming autobiography. I don't think he realised how painful it was for us to "stage his disappearance", as he so gallantly described it. I'll read you one that caught his eye. This quote comes from Haldane's 1927 collection of essays, *Possible Worlds*. He was a Scottish mathematical biologist, of all things – not Elliot's usual source of inspiration, I think you'll agree. "My suspicion is that the universe is not only queerer than we suppose, but even queerer than we can suppose ... I suspect that there are more things in heaven and earth than are dreamed of, or can be dreamed of, in any philosophy.''

'Elliot's mother, Rose, has asked that I read out this little prayer she used to recite to him as a child:

Matthew, Mark, Luke and John
The bed be blest that I lie on.
Four angels to my bed,
Four angels round my head,
One to watch, and one to pray,
And two to bear my soul away.'

As Rose took another petite sip from her brandy, she noticed the lacquered playing-card box with its ivory cribbage board inlaid on the top. That had been her mother's. There were a number of things around the flat that had come from home. She supposed that Blaise would get to keep it all now, unless she asked. Apparently there was some law nowadays that said the partners got everything unless you were prepared to make a fuss – and, typically, Berni had forgotten about the little things in his will.

They say *it's* the same as marriage, but married people don't leave each other for years like Blaise left Berni. Married people don't run around the world and lead separate lives whenever the fancy takes them. And, if some of those things she'd read in Berni's books were actually true, well, married people certainly don't behave like *that*. It's all well and good to play at being grown up and responsible when the idea suits, but a shared address and a few flippant endearments do not a marriage make! When you've run a farm with the same husband for forty-five years; when you've had two children by him and cooked a billion meals for your family; when you've done without new clothes for years at a time because the crops were worthless, and used odd balls of wool to knit jumpers – then you're talking marriage.

Even Rose's own struggles weren't sacred. Berni had helped himself to *her* marriage for *his* autobiography. They'd be wanting her to comment on that too, no doubt. There were even hopes of a film. There were always hopes of a film. She'd never been to see the one they made out of *Corpus Delicti*. It never played back home, but if it was anything like the book, Rose would happily give it a wide berth. Apparently, it had been commended at Cannes. Berni had wanted to go but his health hadn't permitted. Now Blaise was selling another film script to another movie company. It just went on and on. There never seemed an end to anything with Berni. Even his death left years of projects in its wake.

'It's a remarkable book, Rose, a beautiful and courageous work.' That's what Sarah Everington, his publisher, said at the funeral. 'I'm so devastated myself to lose Elliot as a friend – a dear one – I just can't imagine how you must feel as his mum.' Sarah had held Rose's hand for a minute, her eyes deep wells of sympathy. She'd even slipped her a card. 'If there's anything we can do, *really*, anything at all, you will call, won't you?' Rose nodded wearily as Sarah vanished in a flurry of silky black gossamer and a cloud of expensive perfume. *Anything at all?* thought Rose. *Well, you could bally well not publish the dashed book, for a start.* But of course that wasn't what Sarah had meant.

'Oh busy you unruly publisher, why dost thou so?' Elliot moaned playfully as Sarah floated by his bedside. Her dark hair shone like fresh liquorice, her red lips were as tempting as steak tartare. He felt like a vampire yearning over the impossible chasm that separated the living from the dead. He desired women and men equally, now that he was no longer a threat or a possibility to either.

'Go chide tardy authors who still hope to make the Christmas list.'

'What, and let my quaint propriety turn to dust? Not on your nelly, Elli.'

'Pages, pages. What do I want from the typesetters now? Can't Blaise look them over?'

'He has, darling. You may as well have something to read while you recuperate.'

'Sarah, I'm not recuperating. I'm dy ...'

'Shoosh, shoosh, shoosh. Ours is a business relationship, after all.'

'Well, I'd never front up to your office looking like this. Dracula without the nocturnal charms. If you won't allow me my Camille, at least let me be Dennis Potter.'

'Exactly. You don't need to watch your life flash before you; you can read it for yourself.'

'I might get delirious and want to change things.'

'Well, you'll have to speak to your agent. No man's rich enough . . .'

'. . . to buy back his own past. I know.'

'But few get to make quite the industry out of it that you have, dearie.'

'Nonsense. I usually write fiction – you know that.'

'That's what I thought until a certain Blaise person began representing you a couple of years back. I'm not usually a woman given to blushing but a certain wordsmith of ours wasn't always one hundred per cent honest, was he?'

'Honest, schmonest. You got your filthy lucre back. I got Blaise back. No one's complaining, no one went to court. A good time was had by all.'

After my mother, Dinah Carrisbush was my first love. She possessed all the big-city glamour a dirt-bowl town like Nguurrambang lacked. She played the latest records, wore all the hippest gear. In rural New South Wales in the early 1970s that was enough to keep a smouldering town's lazy eyes on you. Dinah had a way about her that caused peek-a-boo tremors in lace curtains and diamond partings in venetian blinds. She taught me how to dance to songs like *The Love Bug, Good Morning Starshine,* and *I Am Woman.* We had something groovy going on.

Under purple summer sunsets we'd dance around her sun-scorched yard, her topaz cat on the verandah and a matching two-tone Holden FB in the drive. She told me about Sydney and how you could dance all night at some places. You could have drinks in hollowed-out pineapples and go to parties in the shortest mini-skirt – no one even cared. Dinah wore scarves and shiny lace-up boots. She had midis and maxis and sunglasses like a movie star. She drank long cold drinks with lemon, ice and vodka in them. She worked in the Wilma Edmonds's dress shop on Ray Street. And Dinah was the only woman who ever drank in the bar at the Nguurram pub.

Elsie MacPherson worked in the bar of the Nguurram pub. She'd have been the first to start the rumours about Dinah, and you can guarantee Wilma Edmonds would be the first to listen. When Marie Hislop got wind of them, she drove her Ford Futura into town – and there was a showdown that February afternoon. I could see the red dirt she kicked up a full kilometre away at our place. It was as if Dinah vanished from my life in the same cloud of red dust that Marie Hislop left in her wake. When Marie came a-calling with murder in her eyes, Dinah knew the town wasn't big enough for both of them. I never knew the full story, which is strange. Secrets didn't keep well in a town like that. They curdled like milk in the sun and you could smell them for miles – a rancid mess no one wanted to clean up.

Mum reckoned Dinah had some bloke in Sydney, but I couldn't see why Marie would have cared about that. Mum said other things too. 'Marie Hislop couldn't afford to be turning her back on her Ron – it wasn't the first time he'd played up and it wouldn't be the last – but that Dinah Carrisbush had no business going into that pub on her own, anyway. Skimpy frocks and fancy drinks. She was asking for trouble.' Mum maintained that the Dinah Carrisbushes of this world were better off somewhere like Sydney because there were dozens of bars they could go to and a million dress shops they could work in. I'd spend afternoons dreaming about Dinah in some Sydney boutique – a smart one where pop stars or TV personalities might go, maybe even a department store. I'd run away and join her there one day. She'd be waiting, I knew she would.

After she'd left town I used to speculate about what she'd be doing. I'd picture her swinging her handbag and looking up at the skyscrapers the way Mary Tyler Moore did on her TV show. I'd wonder if she'd go home after work and change into something more comfortable and slinky, or if she looked so smart all day that she could just go straight to one of those bars on her way home. I fantasised about her sipping cocktails perched on a stool, with her lovely legs crossed and her high heels swinging to some groovy music. I knew that Dinah, like Mary Tyler

Moore, was doing it *her* way and she was going to make it, after all.

I knew there'd be nicer blokes to buy her drinks in the city. I imagined Dinah smiling at handsome men – and then I tried to imagine their handsomeness. I found it sometimes in the tear-out advertisements in Mum's *Reader's Digests* or on TV commercials. Men who wore tight flares and platform shoes, and sported sideburns. Men with super-white teeth smiling out of magazines at TAA hostesses who smiled right back, or guys modelling underwear in Grace Bros advertisements. Men who might deserve my lovely Dinah.

Dinah left me her Helen Reddy single. I knew *I Am Woman* off by heart. It wasn't a good song for a thirteen-year-old boy to sing in a place like Nguurrambang, nor did it reflect the mood of the local girls. Feminism tended to bypass towns like mine with the same speed as the super rigs on the highway. So I moped dejectedly around town or hung about in the kitchen, eating Mum's cakes and pestering her with questions about Sydney. She and Dad had been there for their honeymoon in 1960. In the absence of anyone else's stories, it was Mum's I relied on to embellish or consolidate my fantasies.

'So did you go to those bars with Dad, Mum?'

'What bars, love?'

'The ones you reckon Dinah can go to. Did you ever drink out of a pineapple or a coconut?'

'Oh, your dad and I have never been big drinkers. We went to a lovely dance at the Manly town hall and took a nice ferry ride. And we went to the Easter Show, so we could see some grain-processing machinery your father was keen to use out back.'

I sighed heavily, slumping my head into my folded arms on the kitchen table. *Farm machinery!* Didn't they have any sense of romance?

'Are you wise, Mum, is your wisdom born of pain? What do you think about Women's Lib?'

She looked up from the sink, her eyes surveying the paddocks, the crops – and Kelly, our mangy dog tethered to the back fence. She paused from her peeling. A perfect spiral of potato skin hung from her motionless hand.

'Well, Wilma Edmonds reckons she's still selling just as many bras and with the price of underwear these days, you'd be a fool to go burning them willy-nilly. That Germaine Thingummy's just a stirrer if you ask me,' she began to wave the peeler at me enthusiastically. 'And when a married man like the deputy prime minister can gallivant publicly with his Asian secretary then things have gone too far . . . set the table for us will you love?'

I decided there and then that I wanted to be a stirrer just like Germaine Thingummy. I wanted to have affairs like Junie Morosi and I wanted to sit in a bar like Dinah Carrisbush – legs a-swinging, music playing and a summer breeze blowin' through the jasmine in my mind.

'Rose?'

'Yes, love.' Rose had been daydreaming. A lass with a shaved head and jewellery in her face was talking to her up close. Rose could see the girl was pretty enough, and wondered why on earth she didn't let her hair grow out. If she bought herself something more feminine to wear she'd be very attractive indeed. Rose learnt that the girl's name was Freya and that she'd been Berni's *carer* towards the end of his illness. At least she was helping herself to some of Rose's cake.

'That cake is fabulous. My mum never cooked cakes like this.'

'Oh, it was Berni's favourite. That's a shop-bought one, though. I never like the icing unless I make it myself. They tell you now not to give sweet things to kids, but he always loved my baking. Hollow legs, Berni had.' She laughed at the memory. Freya sat beside her, nibbling the sponge.

'I'm so glad you got down here, you know, before the end. At least the two of you could talk.'

'Yes . . . didn't seem to be a lot to say, just remembering childhood and his dad, God love him. Berni's way of life wasn't the sort of thing you'd prattle about in Nguurrambang.'

'But you must be proud, he was always challenging that.

God, he went out to schools in the country to explain that there was a future for kids who didn't know how to deal with their sexuality.' Freya's brow furrowed with earnestness. 'Have you any idea, Rose, how many kids in rural areas commit suicide because of their sexuality? The papers won't admit that's the reason, but there are some really dangerous assumptions about sexuality and masculinity in our society. It's even worse in rural areas.'

Rose was gripping her handbag ever more tightly with the sting of the words. Freya was making her uncomfortable, she really didn't know what to say.

'Please. It's my son's funeral. I'm not here to be lectured about the sins of country life. There's plenty of room for improvement in the city, if you ask me.'

'Oh Rose, I'm sorry. I wasn't trying to lecture you. I just wanted you to know how proud everyone was of the stuff Elliot achieved in those areas.'

'*Everyone*,' muttered Rose under her breath.

'He even went back to his own old school, didn't he?'

Rose made a whimpering sound, then sniffled into her handkerchief. She looked at Freya, her chin trembling.

'Yes, he did. And I couldn't show my face in the town for a month afterwards. He didn't ask his father or me. Never bothered to think how it would affect us. I had to get my groceries delivered, and the shame of it was probably what put a stop to his dad's heart in the end.' She paused miserably. 'Oh, Berni loved to jump up and down –

make a lot of noise, gay-bally-this, rights-for-that, I want, I want, gimmee, gimmee. You don't need to tell me what he *did*, Freya, I listened to it for *twenty* bloody years!'

Freya went to speak, but Rose was just getting started.

'And what were the rights for? You tell me – books so full of filth and drugs it breaks a mother's heart to read them!' She paused for breath. 'He was diagnosed with HIV when he was thirty, for goodness' sake. He'd tell me it's not a gay disease, but do you know anyone who's got it who isn't? And what about the drugs and all-night parties where the Lord himself would weep to know what went on? I'll tell you one thing, rights for that sort of carry-on are going to be a long time coming and not something decent people – country *or* city – are going to be putting up with in a hurry.'

Freya had no idea what she'd started. Now she didn't know how to stop it.

'It was us who let him run off to university and fill his head with all that business, though I don't suppose there would have been anything for him back home. Dead at forty-four, that's what he got for his trouble. Plenty of them died younger with that dreadful AIDS. And as for being proud! I loved my son – any fit mother does, but the life he chose isn't something a woman of my background could ever be *proud* of. Doors can be closed for a reason, and what goes on behind them is not for public viewing. As far as I'm concerned there are certain things you just don't speak about.' She opened her bag for some more Kleenex. 'Lord knows we didn't have to talk about sex all the time in my day. Sex is a very private thing – people got on with it without books and university courses and whatnot.' She began to sob quietly. Freya didn't feel qualified to comfort her, given that she'd set her off to begin with, but offered what clichéd solace she could.

'A good cry, now that's what you need.' Rose nodded, her face collapsing into a pillow of tissues.

Blaise arrived at the scene and put his arm around Rose. 'What's Freya-the-Brave been doing to you?' He winked at Freya, who was a little weepy herself at the mess she'd created.

Rose coughed, 'It's not her fault. I'm just . . . getting too old for all this grief, Blaise. It was his father two years ago.' Her glistening eyes met with Blaise's. 'Oh, it would have been good if his brother, Des, could have come over from Perth. They never really got on, Berni and Des. Chalk and cheese, but he should have been here for me.'

'Oh Rose, I know. There just weren't any seats on a flight.'

Blaise was quietly relieved that Des wasn't present. He was Berni's antithesis. He would have been like a fish out of water at this gathering.

'Mind you, I don't know what he'd make of all this.' She gazed around the crowded flat.

'You're still not sure what to make of it, are you Rose?'

She looked up at Blaise, who sat on the arm of the chair in a pose that suggested he was the parent and she the child.

'Grief seems to make children of us all, Rose.'

'I think it's even worse than that for me. You're not supposed to outlive your children. The Lord equips you for your parents' passing but not your children's.' She sniffled. 'I'd have sooner He took me. I'd have been ready to go now.'

'Nonsense, you've got years left. I suppose it really is Berni's day. He did tell me he'd never make old bones, but I always took it with a pinch of salt. I somehow thought he'd bury us all with his sheer bloody-mindedness. Always liked a fuss being made, didn't he?'

Rose chuckled, forced a smile and dabbed her eyes. 'The bigger the better.'

Blaise grinned back as Freya took her leave. 'Don't worry about Freya. She didn't mean to upset you.'

'I know she didn't, love. It's a different world here.'

Different was right. At home you didn't have *carers*. Friends and neighbours helped out where they could and June Horsley, the district nurse, popped in on her daily rounds. It wasn't the AIDS that killed Berni in the end – that's what the doctor had told her. He'd said the steroids Berni used to take to stop the weight loss, and the other medication, had taken their toll. They'd put a strain on his liver and it packed it in. 'He shouldn't have been drinking like he has been these last few years, either,' the doctor had added, to further indemnify himself. Rose thought he was splitting hairs about the AIDS. After all, if he hadn't had the wretched thing to begin with, he wouldn't have been taking the drugs in the first place.

'At least I glimpsed the next century, Mum – it's not so special. Just more of the same, really. Sorry to have been such a worry,' Berni had said as she sat by his bed. She hadn't known what to say.

He'd picked up the library book she had been reading while he was asleep. 'Maeve Binchy: *Circle of Friends*, I bet you wish I wrote books like this, hey, Mum? Too bad I wasn't Bryce Courtenay or Catherine Cookson; do you forgive me?'

'Oh stop it, you.' She put the book back in her lap. 'I sometimes used to think the goblins had given us a changeling with you, son. I wondered whether some hippy mob in the city ended up with a boy who looked just like you but was the complete opposite – never read a book, chased girls and tinkered with cars and tractors all the time.'

Berni was hardly listening. He was dozing off while she stroked his hair. There wasn't much left of it now: blond, brown and grey wisps barely covering his scalp. He would have gone completely bald like her father if he'd . . . Well, there was no point in wishing for what wasn't to be, was there? His skin was yellow, his cheekbones so sharp now they looked painful. The nurse said he had very little liver function left and that he was relying on a drip for nourishment and rehydration. The doctor maintained *it* wouldn't be long. They kept checking his feet – that's how they could tell, circulation. It seemed so morbid, but for Rose a life on the farm had made nature's cruelties mundane. She went back to reading her book. *How strange to read a book while waiting for your son to die*, she'd thought, as his breaths audibly lessened in strength. 'A mother's love is a balm for life, a blessing from God through trouble and strife.' She remembered that poem from one of her *Friendship Books* or *Fireside Annuals* full of lovely thoughts for every day of the year. But where was the mother's balm? From whence comes her strength?

'I still like *Intra Venus* best,' said one of the men in a nearby conversation cluster.

'Oh God, I hated that. I never had the heart to tell Elliot. You can't with friends, can you? It was just *sooo* pretentious.'

'And *we* could never be accused of that, could we, dear?

'Speak for yourself. *Je Louse* was my favourite.'

'Don't say that near Blaise or you'll lose an eye. You

only liked it because you were in it, you vain queen.'

'Nonsense. I swear I was in *Corpus Delicti* as well.'

'I thought that transvestite who lived in a permanent K-hole reminded me of someone.'

'Ha ha. That was her name, wasn't it? Kay Hole. God, remember all that Special K and that trip to hospital when we were gaga from GBH – what a nasty little drug *du jour* that turned out to be. Martyrs to pharmaceutical advancement all of us, and were we ever thanked? Were we FUCK! Still, beatifications are always posthumous. It's a wonder all of us have lived this long.'

'Not all of us have, sweetness. Now we're middle-aged zombies who rely on liquor and the kindness of strange GPs – those sweet, gentle souls who can see beyond our perfectly controlled exteriors into the shocking serotonin depletions we've sustained in our perpetual pursuit of chemically charged merriment. I always hoped I'd grow out of it. Not much of a life, is it?'

'Elliot's lucky. He shall not wither, like those of us who remain. He's headed straight for heaven's backroom.'

'Half his licentious luck. Perhaps Elliot has died for our sins, just as Christ allegedly did.' Someone laughed. 'Uumm no, lovely thought – but he died for his own, just as we surely will. The days of that sort of magnanimity are well behind us.'

The trio paused for a moment to look at some photographs.

'But *really*, I think *Gridiron* was his greatest achievement, truly underrated. So raw and unfettered, but I suppose things were in those days.'

They all giggled.

'You know I've never so much as read the cover, but I believe Blaise to be in possession of one solitary copy.'

'Elliot was always terribly coy about it. I imagine because it was such an early work. At twenty, or whatever age he was, one hasn't quite figured out just how much one should reveal in one's work.'

'Well, let's face it, it was the perfect entrée into America and it did gain him *considerable* exposure over there as a young man.'

Rose took a little more brandy. *Gridiron* – now that didn't ring any bells with her, though she remembered him going on that trip. He'd just finished his degree at the university. He was doing modelling in those days – hairdressers, shoe shops, even something for the *New Idea*, she seemed to recall. She still had some pictures. She'd never thought much of the photos he'd sent her. He'd looked a little too full of himself. Vanity in a woman was one thing, but in a man it was an unattractive attribute. Modelling never seemed a proper thing for a man to be doing, even if it was just for the money. They weren't the sort of photos a mother liked to have of her son. Des had seen them and said, straight out, 'He's a horse's hoof, that Berni.'

She'd jumped right down his throat. 'Don't you talk that way about your brother!' But it was at that time it dawned on her that Des might just be right. Rose put the pictures in the sideboard drawer. She didn't want his father seeing them. There'd been talk enough about Marie Hislop's daughter. She could do without all that.

Elliot had a chemical taste in his mouth. Blaise had just kissed him, quite generously, as he left – and Elliot couldn't help wondering what his breath was like. TV, books: when you were this sick, it was hard to engage with either. Illness and game-shows just didn't mix – hell with flashing lights and low-cut evening gowns. Nor did literature and Maxalon. Imagery, however eloquent, became nauseating. He'd sneered at his mother's reading tastes, but the gentle love and kindness found in her sorts of novels was all he could really stomach now.

The liver filters the drugs that might have helped – but once it's gone off-line, nothing works properly anymore. Except morphine. Morphine always works, the last human resort. 'The Bahamas, Club Med, last stop Morphine.' He giggled to himself. Mum would be in later, so he'd read some more of his book now, before she arrived. Patient Mum, steadfast Mum. *So why hide the autobiography from her? Why not let her read and respond?* 'Because I'm a coward,' thought Elliot, 'because I'm dying, because it's true and because little boys don't like their mummies to be mad at them. Disappointed by them.

Adolescence stretches itself out like a jewelled snake on a burning riverbank. Long and dangerous. Each nerve end exposed to every stimulus. A serpent always ready to thrash itself into a heated frenzy or shrivel like a raisin. If I hadn't been a little monster in that environment, if I hadn't had the monstrous will to survive, I would have hanged myself in the shed where the thresher was kept. I would have swung and creaked in the wind like the vacancy sign outside Bert and Carol Hamley's motel on Boomerang Street. 'When you stay with the Hamleys, you're staying with family' read the sign.

Bert and Carol gave me my first job. I used to skim scum from the compact, kidney-shaped pool, gathering leaves, dragonflies and other summer bug-life which accrued in the tempting, but fatal, blue shallows. I'd watch station-wagon parents supervise their kids in a poolside playground with white, wrought-iron furniture and painted car-tyre planters wittily cut into the shape of swans. The guests were all people who came from someplace else, on their way to who knows where. That's all our town was – a pit-stop, a piss-stop, a dumping ground for ice-cream wrappers, apple cores and chip packets. A place to let radiators hiss and bubble, or to clean grubby kids' faces with Wet-Ones and dispose of smelly, loaded nappies.

Litter and flies were all anyone ever brought into Nguurrambang. Speeding cars full of stink.

'You'd wonder why they'd bother driving another fifty kilometres to Coopers Creek,' Bert would say. 'There's bloody nothin' there. They'll pay the same for a room and they won't get the colour tellies.' I'd nod in agreement, as my rake sifted artificially coloured gravel. 'They must be out of their minds, Bert. Out of their bloody minds.'

Des and I would nag Mum and Dad to buy a colour telly but things were always tight. Dad said if you want colour you can use your imagination – after all, they'd had to in the fifties, when life seemed like it truly was black and white. 'Berni's got his head in the clouds or in a book most of the time anyway and there's plenty of work to be done out back if Des gets bored and wants to keep himself in pocket money.'

Dad didn't even ask me to help anymore. I'd proven a hopeless farmhand. I cried as a child when he shot rabbits. We'd traipse across endless paddocks, our whole primeval family hunting together. Me, moaning and tripping on tussocks, slipping down burrows, my gumboots forever too large. 'There might be snakes . . . I'm tired . . . it's too muddy . . . it's too cold . . . you're going too fast . . .' What a pathetic wimp I must have been. Even I would have hated me if I'd been my father.

Our bucolic treks were bleak adventures indeed. Shots were fired, rabbits darted and the victorious shooter would pick up the twitching, wounded trophy and wring its neck as perfunctorily as Mum would wring a sopping dishcloth. Cliiiick, and there it lay. Warm, long, furry and dead.

It didn't end there. Then the gutting wanted doing. The furs needed to be hung out to dry. I was squeamish about that, too. Though I'll never know why, given the things I've done since – virtually turned one or two men inside out, with little more than a whimper to mark the occasion. Perhaps it was because I left them alive that they thrilled me so. No taste for the kill, me.

I was always clumsy with tasks allotted to me on the farm – and, in time, I'm sure Dad was afraid to be alone with me, his kid from outer space. I don't know whether he loved me, but he certainly didn't like me. I wished I could be a girl. No one expected a girl to fix a tractor or a car but if she did, she'd enjoy a certain rarefied notoriety among the blokes. A man who made a cake needed to be in possession of great inner fortitude. Of course some girls went too far, like Bronnie Hislop, whose tomboy antics and filthy mouth caused her mother, Marie, to have a nervous disorder. But if a girl was good, hardworking, sweet, pretty and didn't open her legs too wide too many times for too many blokes, she'd do alright. I ached to be one of those girls. I'd have been sweet, *really* I would. Unless one of the spunks like Col Turner, David Musgrove or Gavin Peppertree had wanted to finger me, in which case I would have drunk a bottle of blackberry nip and then made like I couldn't remember a thing afterwards. The world would vanish into a pool of purple vomit and I'd be left with nothing but a fuzzy head and a filthy reputation – a stain like beetroot on the red earth, a curse as deadly as the pointed bone to a fast-beating heart.

Teresa came and sat by Rose.

'How are you going, Rose?'

'Oh . . . you know, love. I might help myself to another brandy in a minute.'

'I would if I were you, this lot don't seem to be holding back.' And she was right. The guests were getting more intemperate as the day progressed. Rose felt invisible where she sat on the couch. She preferred it that way.

'Do you remember a book of Berni's called *Gridiron*, Teresa?'

'A book . . . ah . . . no, though he probably did plenty of work that I never saw. Rose, are you still doing your cross-stitch and embroidery?'

Rose chuckled. 'Not much else for me to do, though my eyes give me a bit of gip. The farm's all sold off now, so I like to do toys and stuff for the littlies – things they can sell at church fêtes and CWA fundraisers.'

'I should get you to do another series of birds or insects. Claudia still has the gallery, you know.'

Rose laughed again, 'Eight hundred dollars each for

those! Who'd have thought it?' *Was it five years ago?* pondered Rose.

It was shortly after Berni's final return from America, the last year of a century she'd never imagined outliving. Berni, Blaise and Teresa had visited Rose in Nguurrambang – a rarity, to say the least. They had been on their way through to a festival in Adelaide and had stopped to take in the view from nearby Sugarloaf Mountain. It seemed to Rose that they had festivals for just about anything these days, and the gays didn't go without their share of them. Teresa had been praising the countryside and mountains in a way that only passers-through ever did. And while Rose never imagined living anywhere else, she was always a little suspicious when city visitors were too enthusiastic. Teresa had been fascinated by Rose's needlepoint. Rose had thought her patronising with all her effusive praise.

'Rose, this work is exquisite. You should sell it.'

'Oh, love, I just do it for myself and the church fete. That fabric used to line my best coat, but I haven't worn it for I wouldn't like to think how many years. Never usually work on black. Not very cheery, is it?'

'Black never needs an excuse, Rose.' Teresa picked up an embroidery frame with a magnificent filigree dragonfly embroidered onto fragile black satin in golds, yellows and subtle shades of brown. She poked through the sewing basket and found two others, a caterpillar and a butterfly, on the same satin.

'These are beautiful . . . Rose, do you think I could show them to a friend of mine? She might be able to exhibit them for you.'

'It's not worth the bother, love. The frames would cost more than the work's worth.'

'I think you'd be surprised.'

Rose was embarrassed but couldn't see the harm in it, so Teresa took her 'scraps' away with her.

Six months later, Rose had completely forgotten about them. Berni was on the phone saying, 'Mum, you're coming to Sydney. I've bought you a train ticket.' He wouldn't tell her what it was about. Just that it was a surprise, and that she'd be going out for dinner and staying with him and Blaise. She hadn't liked to leave her husband, Bob, by himself. He got cranky if he had to fix his own tea, but she'd sat herself on the train for four-and-a-half hours and they'd been waiting for her at Central.

'What's all this about, Berni?' she'd said as they whisked her off in the car.

'We wanted to take you out for dinner, for Mother's Day.'

'But Mother's Day was months ago. You sent me that

lovely bouquet. I dried the cornflowers that came in it – they're in Des's old room now.' Berni was good with presents – always sending gifts and expensive knick-knacks, but it was time with him she yearned for. Sadly, it was time he never seemed able to afford.

'Well it's your *real* Mother's Day, Mum. We're taking you to a gallery opening in Paddington and then out for dinner.'

'A gallery opening, goodness. I've not been to one of those before. I hope it's not too mad and modern for your old Mum.'

'It's an exhibition of great, undiscovered Australian women artists,' said Teresa in a nonchalant, professional tone. 'There are exhibits across all mediums.'

Rose looked at Teresa. She had no idea what a medium was unless it was to do with a séance. 'Is it one of these feminist dos?'

'Not at all, Rose. We just wanted you to see a couple of the works before we took you to dinner. Someone very dear to your Berni has some pieces in it.'

Rose had felt rather underdressed when she'd arrived. She'd worn one of her church frocks, the one she'd bought at Wilma Edmonds' closing-down sale, and she'd chosen a dark cardigan that matched her bag. They were offered champagne on their arrival and Berni promptly introduced his mother to Claudia, the svelte curator who commandeered the event.

'Rose, what a delight that you've gone to the trouble of coming to Sydney. We're so thrilled to have *you* in the gallery.' She moved closer to Rose and whispered into her ear, 'Has he been keeping you locked away in Nguurrambang for fear of competition?'

Rose couldn't begin to guess what the woman was suggesting.

'Come on, Rose,' said Blaise, snatching a mini-pizza from the roaming tray. And she was whisked off, past blurred landscapes, surreal portraits, sculptures and collages. There were some lovely things, to be sure, and the champagne was a treat she was quite unused to. She'd had nothing but a sandwich on the train – *and didn't they sting you for that!* – so the alcohol was going straight to her head. They passed into another room, a stark room with only three pieces on display.

'Mum, what do you think of these?' Rose adjusted her glasses and moved towards the gilt frames suspended on the wall. She squinted for a moment. 'Oh, good heavens,' she cried, blushing in shock.

Her three samples had been put back onto round embroidery frames, as if they were still works in progress. The ragged edges of the satin had been smoothed out and each of the works sat perfectly behind glass, floating in square shallow boxes with lovely tarnished black and gold frames. There was nothing else on the entire wall. Surprise and joy filled her eyes with tears, as she read the neatly typed card announcing her exhibit: *Captured Sugarloaf Splendours*, by Rose Elliot.

'Who's the artist *now*, Mum?' She was almost speechless, she reached into her bag for a hanky to blow her nose.

'How did they get in here?' Teresa appeared at Rose's side.

'Claudia offers her gallery once a year for this exhibition of works from all over the country. It's funded by the Arts Council, which offers three prizes. Out of over two thousand entries, only fifty are on display.'

'No,' said Rose, her shock replaced by bewilderment.

'I've some bad news though, Mum.'

'What?'

'You didn't win the competition.'

'Well, of course, I wouldn't . . .'

'You came third.'

'Lord, no!'

'Only fifteen hundred dollars prize money for you, I'm afraid.'

'You're having me on . . .'

'There's good news too, Mum.' Rose didn't know where to look. Berni was stringing her along. Teasing her like he used to when she didn't have a clue about some latest thing or other. But she didn't mind. Her heart was racing. She felt like a girl: a wild, young, reckless girl of twenty. She hadn't felt so alive in . . . in years.

'The good news is that the gallery will take those old

bits of fête fodder off your hands for eight hundred bucks a piece.'

She brought her handkerchief to her face, smiling so broadly her cheeks ached. Fair bursting with jubilation.

'I'll have to get myself one of those women you've got, Berni. Who are they? Agents!'

'I'm so proud of you, Mum.' Berni put his arm around his mother as they both regarded her work.

There was a powerful flash. They turned to face a photographer from the *Wentworth Courier*. Rose's most radiant smile was preserved forever, just as her *Sugarloaf Splendours* had been.

She could see that photograph now. It was up on the board with all the other snaps of Berni at different ages and stages. Rose wondered if that time in Sydney hadn't been one of the happiest days in her life. She'd been sixty-five then. She had no longer expected to experience such happiness as that. It had been the most memorable and perfect day. Berni gave it to her. Berni and Teresa. Berni who had demanded so much from everyone all his life, who'd tired her out, who'd forced her into the role of messenger for every fresh atrocity and scandal he delivered. The awful tales she'd had to tell his father and brother. The still-more-dreadful things she'd had to hide.

'If they can't cope with a homo, then bugger them,'

had been Berni's attitude. He made it so difficult. Thinking back now, she wished the Lord could have taken her shortly after that day at the gallery. Taken her with a smile on her face and wicked, glorious pride in her heart.

'Good for you, love,' Bob had said when she returned with her prize and an uncommon flush of urbane confidence. 'Good on ya, Rose. Mind you, they've got more money than sense, those Sydney types.'

Her exuberance waned as quickly as it had waxed. She couldn't make her husband see how important it had been, how many people were at the gallery and how she had a whole white wall to herself, with special individual lights shining on each of her 'works'. That's what they called them there: fine works, great works. Berni sent the picture from the paper, she showed it to Marie Hislop and Wilma Edmonds – both of whom, despite failing health, could still spread a bit of worthwhile gossip about town. They'd been thrilled, of course, but they couldn't know what it was like for her. For her to feel proud. 'It's not what you know, but who you know,' Wilma had said over their cuppa – and Rose sank a little further into the ordinary, the duck who'd thought itself a swan. She reminded herself about modesty, about the tall poppies that get the snip. Rose had always known pride as a sin, the dizzy moment before a terrible fall. When she had felt so good on that day, so proud, it crossed her mind that even if it was a sin, she didn't really give a tuppenny shrug. She'd started to wonder of late whether all her sacrifices had been worthwhile. The church always taught it. Sacrifice. So what business did she have wanting? The song of want was played on the Devil's pipe, and it was a tune she'd tried not to dance for. No good ever came of it.

Rose's moment of pride bought her a dishwasher and a new tumble dryer, and why shouldn't she have them after years of slog? Perhaps the Lord never really expected as much of her as she thought. If her greatest creations were a couple of embroideries and two sons, wasn't that enough? *Well it better had be, because that was all he was getting.* She had a quick laugh, then settled back satisfied. There was a courage to be had from the brandy, after all.

If she'd passed on before her husband, she might have missed her great moment of artistic triumph – and this, her terrible sadness, the death of one of her sons. Now there would be only Des to bid her off when the time came. She was lucky if she saw him twice a year. His wife, Jennifer, wasn't quite the sort of girl Rose had hoped for as a daughter-in-law, and the grandchildren barely know their nanna. *I bet he could have got on a plane if he'd really tried. They give special consideration if there's been a death in the family.* Rose knew that because Mavis McClure had got a ticket to Sydney when her sister passed away – and that had been during the Olympics when there weren't tickets to be had for love nor money. Rose gulped a mouthful of drink angrily, a frown descending upon her brow as she considered the possible treachery involved. *I bet that Jennifer had a hand in it – moaned about the cost is my guess. Jennifer would rather new curtains in the lounge than have Des flying off to Sydney for his own brother's funeral.* 'I've had enough of it!' Rose gasped, she'd spoken out loud but no one seemed to notice, not with all the other voices and their raucous pronouncements.

Des's lot were too busy with their jobs, kids and new house, so they couldn't get to her very often, and Rose hated planes – or at least she knew she would if she ever got on one. Three days on the train to Western Australia she just couldn't come at. You never imagine life will pick people up and take them so far away – Perth, New York. Your own children moving as far away as possible. *What have they got in those places that could make a family scatter so?* It just didn't seem fair. She sighed. 'All God's children have walking shoes,' she remembered from somewhere in the Bible, or from a lost sermon during her youth. She supposed grief to be another of her lessons but it was an enormous burden and it had worn her down. The Lord seemed to save his biggest tests and greatest cruelties until you'd no spirit or strength left to bear them. *Life all seems back-to-front*, she thought quietly.

Reincarnation. Berni went on about that, but she didn't fancy the idea. 'Heaven'll do me nicely, if they'll have me,' she'd said to Berni during one of their hospital conversations.

'I'm sure they will, Mum. There'll be a lovely room filled with all your handiwork and a prime view of Sugarloaf Mountain. What about me? What if I have to come back? The Hindus say you come through the same family time and time again. God, I don't want to be Des and Jennifer's third child.' Rose laughed.

'Well they're not having any more, Jen's nearly forty and she's had her hands full with little Carter. He's a cheeky fellow, just like his father.'

'Well, see that they don't, will you? I can't take any chances.' Berni laughed too. 'If I thought I was going to be reborn to them I'd leave myself some money to escape with. That would be a scream, wouldn't it, leaving money to someone who hasn't even been born yet?'

'Oh, your brother's not so bad, you could do worse.'

Rose hadn't had her seventieth birthday yet but was feeling and looking older, or perhaps this was how you were supposed to feel. For Rose, vanity was a vice she had never truly mastered, and one long banished by work and worry. 'The only reason people notice a woman of my age is because they're neighbours and they're expected to be polite or because they're unemployed hooligans who'd steal your purse as quick as look at you.'

'Would you like something to eat, Mrs Elliot?'

The pretty blonde lass from the caterers was in front

of her with a tray of fried Oriental goodies. She didn't know if she dared. She still had something from earlier stuck between her teeth and fried food did tend to make her stomach play up. She took one anyway. Her brandy was gone – again. She quite fancied another and asked the girl if she might fetch it for her. She donned her glasses to go and inspect the photo board Blaise had arranged with all sorts of memories, trophies and newspaper articles. Blaise helped her up as he passed. Her balance seemed a bit off-kilter.

'Don't worry about me, love, you've your guests to attend to.'

'They're quite capable of looking after themselves.'

'Blaise?'

'Yes, Rose.'

'What's this *Gridiron* of Berni's? I heard some of the fellows talking about it, sounded like something he wrote in America, when he first went out there.'

'Oh, that . . . that was just a joke thing he did. It was way before I came onto the scene. I think it was kind of a gay guide to the gridiron teams they have in the States.'

'I'm surprised he would have done a guide like that. He never took the slightest interest in sport. I would have thought rugby or football far too . . . rough for my Bernard.'

'I suppose it was the money, it was probably too good to refuse. One of the magazines he wrote for would have asked him to do it or something.'

'Someone said you had a copy here.'

'God,' Blaise rested his finger on his lips in deep contemplation. 'I might but goodness knows where. I'll send it to you if I find it. It wouldn't mean a thing to me – I don't know any of the players myself.'

'I wonder why that fellow was calling it his best work.'

'Oh, Rose, you know what these guys are like. Full of sarcasm.' Full of poison too, some of them, he thought but didn't say. 'I'm sure they were just having a joke.'

'Well they did seem to be laughing.' Yes, Blaise was right, they were joking about it.

Rose followed the trail of pictures around the board. There was one of her nursing Berni on the front porch – she'd crocheted that blanket herself. There was Berni on the tractor eating his Vegemite on bread, Berni and Dinah Carrisbush – in colour – on the front of Dinah's old Holden – he's wearing some of her hippy gear and sunglasses. Berni and Bronnie, Marie Hislop's girl, dangling their legs off the back of Marie's station wagon tailgate. There was only one picture of his dad. Berni was just as handsome as his dad, though he made more of himself than his father ever had. Berni's 'lot' did tend to go in for the fancy clothes and what have you.

'Poor old Dad. I haven't given you much of a show in this bio', have I?' Elliot squeezed the morphine pack. They were letting him have as much as he liked now. A wave of sentimental remorse came over him. That's why he hadn't wanted to go through the pages – again. Sarah thought of it as occupational therapy, but his occupation was nearly done. Reparation kept going through his mind, the word littering his dreams. Strange dreams about being in a hospital, a repatriation hospital, and his dad already being there. Not a grumpy, distracted dad but a smiling one. Dad after a couple of beers. Dad fixing his bike when he couldn't do it. Dad dropping him off at Dinah's and nudging him about having a girlfriend. 'Better watch it with Dinah, Berni, she'd be the fast type, I reckon.' Elliot felt a tear and blinked it back. Maybe his dad hadn't been so uninterested after all. Perhaps he hadn't been having a go at him all those times. Maybe it had been him all along. Determined to be isolated, needing to feel wounded. He wondered if he'd the strength to type more words, be more generous. To give his dad a name. To admit that Robert was his father. He wondered why country people went in for such fine old dignified names when they were only ever used as contractions – Bob, Berni.

My old man never beat me or sexually abused me or got drunk and said weird things. I don't remember seeing anything especially nasty in the woodshed or being made to hold my water or dragged screaming to some brothel where painted ladies made fearless men out of spotty country lads. My father ignored me mostly, which may be even worse.

I remember him saying I was 'as much use as a girl', and whether he said it only once or a dozen times, it seemed to burn itself into my mind like a mantra.

Des was younger than me, but he got the hang of the tractor earlier. Des was the gifted one as far as Dad was concerned. I was more of a mummy's boy who was lucky his *mummy* indulged him. 'Feminine' tasks, well executed, were never met with quite the ticker-tape parade of adulation that Des received for his mammoth hunts.

Childish career aspirations were another dead give-away. I'd decide to be a hairdresser one year, a cook or a fashion designer the next. I wanted to write plays, even though I'd never seen one. The women would smile with a secret knowledge of what meanings might be construed from these naïve vocational choices.

Oh, the cruel horror. Adults see the calamity of gender way before its rigorous implications ever dawn on one's carefree androgynous baby-psyche. I may never have excelled in the barnyard or the sports field, Dad, but I did play gridiron once – and that was not a girl's game.

Elliot squeezed the pump pack once more. He'd read enough and as he drifted off he thought about reparation, repatriation. 'All care, no responsibility,' he grumbled to himself as the male nurse with curly blond hair and the delicious-looking backside inserted a thermometer into his parched mouth.

You could only see glimpses of the harbour from the windows now. 'Harbour glimpses,' proclaimed Blaise expansively to guests who crowded the small balcony for cigarettes and funereal gossip.

'Half a million for this!' Rose had been incredulous when they'd bought it. She'd been selling farm acres off for five grand apiece. Berni could sing its praises as much as he wanted, but to her it was still a poky two-bedroom flat with a funny little office and a strange laundry-cupboard arrangement. Originally they had a lovely view but after much legal wrangling, a developer had just completed an unsightly monstrosity right in front of them. Their much celebrated aqua-vista was gone.

'Elliot took the view with him, Rose. I don't suppose I'll stay here now. Of course that developer probably took twenty-five per cent off the value too, but what can you do?'

Rose didn't want to talk about money and disbursements with Blaise. People in the city seemed to talk about nothing else, money, property – all a lot of haughty how-do-you-do. It gave her acid. She gazed towards the window. Rose thought the city was a nightmare, and couldn't imagine why anyone would want to live in it. First, there'd been all those tunnels for the Olympic Games, now there were train lines she'd never even heard of on previous trips. She swore they built a dozen new tower blocks between each of her visits. Huge, ugly, precarious-looking things with names people dropped as if the buildings themselves were celebrities. Babelissima, Millennium Manors, 2005, C21. 'Well, we all know what happened to the Tower of Babel,' she thought smugly. This would be her last time in Sydney. No reason to visit again.

Blaise had grown quite plump in the last five years, his cheeks had gone from rosy to ruddy. He'd been no more than a boy when Berni first took up with him. Rose didn't take to him at the start, he had all sorts of tickets on himself and played up the sissy thing more than Berni ever had. But he was older now, and he'd looked after her boy when the chips were down. That's as much as you can ask for. Blaise seemed to swell as Berni shrank. She'd seen her son in August and he looked thin but healthy, hearty even. By Christmas, it looked as if five years had flashed by. Then, in the hospital, even at death's door, he seemed to have turned back into a child. Ageless and ethereal – once again that impish little boy the goblins had given her nearly half a century ago.

He'd been like an actor, Berni. Using that body for whatever new role he wanted to play, treating it like a costume which hadn't been made well enough to endure the demands of its inhabitant. He'd changed it with muscles, long withered now. Tanned it, pierced it and, she suspected, even altered it surgically – though she never got a confession out of him. His ears used to stick out more when he was young and she'd never heard of that improving with age.

'So what *is* going to happen with the apartment?' said one of two happily inebriated men talking in the corner. Rose's ears pricked up. She, too, had almost downed another brandy. She'd shocked herself. *That's one an hour, old girl.* Rose had probably never drunk more than three glasses in a row of anything alcoholic in her life.

'Well, it's all his. Blaise's – lock, stock and manuscript. He hasn't worked for two years now.'

'You don't think Elliot was work?'

'God knows. I thought he'd become a kitten in the last twelve months.'

'It just shows, if you spend long enough with anyone, the tables will eventually turn.'

'I bet I'm one of the only males here who didn't sleep with him, though. You did, didn't you?'

'Yes, a million years ago. The Palaeolithic period, I think it was, when you were still making do with nocturnal emissions in the safety of your mum and dad's suburban home.'

'Safety, huh? I envy Blaise. I want to be a *widow*. Not a divorcee, a widow, it's so much more respectable. A rich one, of course,' he took on a theatrical pose. 'To spend years with someone brilliant, even be mistreated if needs be, but in the end, to clean up the spoils. Look at Blaise, thirty-five, not too old to start over – marry again.'

'He could lose a few kilos but he is mourning, I suppose. He gave Elliot his best years, if you don't count that little hiatus-hernia he had with thingummy. Perhaps a phoenix will rise from the ashes.'

'That's probably what he's mourning – his lost "best" years. And here he is! A literary agent whose own lover is his biggest meal ticket. He has made an art out of patronage. I'll credit him that.'

'Ooh, you *are* a bitch. I think you mean he's made an art out of being patronised. You'll learn there are movers and shakers. Elliot was the mover and Blaise the shaker.' The older one regarded the younger one with a certain mock gravity. 'You rather overestimate Elliot's worth, I fear.'

The 'bitch' turned a toothpick in his mouth and smiled wryly. 'So you never wanted to be the girl who got the most cake then? Speaking of which, I might disgrace myself with a slab of this sponge thing, seeing how it's all that's left.'

Rose didn't like the way some of *them* spoke. It was as if they weren't real people at all – just playing dress-ups. Calling partners 'husbands' in belittling tones or wishing for widowhood, of all things. As if grief could be overcome with fast talk, fancy suits, mourning cars and a pair of expensive sunglasses. It was as if they thought life was an old movie. They couldn't begin to imagine what it was really like.

The older one scoffed at the bitch. 'There was a time when plenty of us were widows. Bitter, forsaken *fraus*, widowed from self-made marriages no one ever credited us with to begin with. It's never a happy time and there *are* easier ways to make a living. Believe me!' He sipped his drink, looked the fellow up and down, then dropped his voice an octave. 'But if it's gold you want, darling, you'd better start digging right away.'

'Mum, then Blaise, then nurse, then doctor. In and out they drift and I haven't made a pass at one.' Elliot smiled in the surgical silence of his private room. The idea of reading was becoming more and more ludicrous. 'I must have been meant to have Blaise and Mum. That people should love me so much means there must be a God – and, with all this drug-induced imagery, everything seems to be going to plan.'

In his mind Elliot could see preparations under way. Tents going up, sails being winched high on huge yachts, sound checks and lightshows and whirring cosmic architecture being reconfigured. *Could all this fuss be because of him?* He smiled. He knew it could. He knew whatever he'd done could be forgiven and all problematic excesses could be debriefed, redefined. 'Where's the boat bound?' Elliot cried in a gruff seafaring tone, as the wind clipped the sail into a flap. A smiling man looked about, his beatified face glowing in the sun as he adjusted the rigging.

'Ecclesia, of course. Wind's fair, sea's flat, smooth sailing ahead.' Elliot squinted from the light. He'd be wanting his sunglasses and Blaise had them in the car. He felt a little stupid having asked about the boat. Of course it was bound for Ecclesia. Where else would it be going on such a day?

There was a time when pop stars made it seem OK not to be sure if you were a boy or a girl but even they, permissive emissaries of my Zeitgeist, didn't confess their sexual ambiguities until the late seventies. Heroes in leather and make-up, glamorous gods who could boast about having no memory of 1975, potential patrons of that ghostly diner, *The Boulevard of Broken Dreams,* all coy about sexuality or daring only to go as far as calling themselves bisexual in that grand *liberal* decade of my teens. I'd stand in front of the mirror and mouth the words to songs that transported me elsewhere. Imagining what people would say if I confessed, simultaneously thrilling and horrifying myself at the sensation it would cause. 'I'm a bi-sex-ual.' 'Hello, I'm a bi-sex-ual.' I imagined getting myself up in platform shoes, a satin shirt and lipstick and announcing it in every shop on Ray Street. I bet I could have told Dinah if she'd stuck around. She would have understood.

If I needed a role model I wouldn't find it in Nguurrambang. I accepted that I might not find it anywhere but I knew, or believed, that in the city there were all-night parties where people danced in cages wearing mini-skirts as high as you like and drank savvy drinks served in hollowed-out pineapples.

'Teresa, love, would you be so kind as to get me another brandy, with a little soda in it this time?'

'Sure, Rose. Are you comfortable?'

'I'm just fine.' Rose had grown very fond of Teresa. She always talked to her as if she was one of her friends.

Teresa was knocking back her own drinks quite fast, Rose noticed.

'You never had any children, did you, Teresa?'

'No, I forgot to. I'm thirty-six now, so I'd be a geriatric mother. That's what they call you after thirty-five. A girl-friend of mine had one a couple of years ago – and that's what the patient record board described her as. She was horrified.'

'You're lucky if they keep you in overnight these days,' muttered Rose. 'Children can be a sorrow as well as a joy. I never thought not to have them, though I was happy to stop at two.'

'Did you talk to Blaise's mum?'

'Yes, she seemed very nice. All these years and it was the first time we met. Berni and Blaise used to do one Christmas with her, then one with us. We'd spoken on the phone but you'd think in fifteen years we'd have gotten to know . . . ah well, I suppose it's different when there aren't the grandkiddies.' Even as she said it, Rose realised there wasn't necessarily much difference. That was part of the sorrow.

'I didn't think the wake would go on quite so long. It's about time a few here got taxis but I don't see them leaving,' offered Terri distractedly.

Rose peered across at a graduation photo. Berni's hair was shaved at the sides but long with blond streaks from the sun or the bottle. She had that photo at home on the mantelpiece, 1981, how young he looked – for all the world like a wholesome Aussie surfing lad. Rose wondered if education would have done anything for her. She'd been so ignorant that when he told her he was doing an arts degree, she expected to see paintings. Every semester he talked about books and history and psychology, without so much as the suggestion of a painting. When she finally asked him during his second year, he roared with laughter. 'Poor Mum!' he howled. 'That's fine arts, you dill.' Berni was the first person Rose knew back home who'd got a degree in anything unrelated to agriculture. Arts, fine arts, he never did explain the difference.

Despite her protestations to the contrary, Rose had read all the books her son wrote. She denied it to Berni's dad – told him not to read them himself because he'd only get into a state. Rose was sure he complied, because he'd never read anything but the *Weekly Times* in all their years of marriage. She'd even bought a book through the church newsletter years ago: *Healthy Sex for a Happy Christian Marriage*. She'd left it lying about in the bedroom when the boys were only young. She'd hoped he might have taken a look and given it some thought. She noticed it was gone one day and wondered if he'd taken it out to his shed to mull over. Months later she discovered it in young Berni's room, with markers in the pages containing discouraging tracts on masturbation, oral sex and the abominable and decidedly unhealthy practice of anal sex. What could a twelve-year-old boy possibly want to know about those things for? She kept her mouth shut, but worried sometimes about how much time he spent round at that Dinah Carrisbush's house. It didn't seem quite right, a woman of thirty taking such an interest in a boy of Berni's age.

He used to come home from Dinah's dancing and singing songs. It'd be Dinah says this and Dinah does that. Rose wondered if Dinah hadn't been giving him liquor. According to Elsie MacPherson, Dinah often arrived at the pub a couple of hours before closing. Elsie said you could tell she already had a few under her belt. Mick O'Shea, who owned the local Buy-Rite supermarket, delivered Dinah's groceries of a Friday – delivered, if you'll pardon me! He said it was nothing out of the ordinary for her to have a couple of bottles of vodka in her order, as well as a dozen longnecks of beer. Well, Dinah didn't even like beer, so someone else must have been around there drinking the stuff. Berni said he never saw anyone, but he was always home in time for his tea – the Devil only knew what went on after that.

Rose sighed. Memories were eating her up, leading her on a merry dance. 'Somewhere between Berni's tea-time and last drinks at the Nguurram pub, Dinah must have found time to get herself in all that trouble.'

Some days were lucid. Some passed in a deluded haze, though Elliot wasn't at all convinced that what he was experiencing was delusion. He had long suspected, even in the prime bloom of health, that drugs and their associated perceptions were as much a part of some divine schematic as anything else. Shifting between states of consciousness and different memories reminded him of how truly fluid everything really was. In life it was impossible to hold a moment or a mood. In dreams, physicality became difficult. Running on the spot, falling. No control. And now a manuscript hovered under his distracted gaze. Something he'd written. Something as far away as a hot summer in Nguurrambang or a chilled gazpacho on Long Island.

> 'What's the matter, Berni – afraid of crocodiles, or are ya sulking about Dinah? *Dinah, Dinah, show us your vagina . . .*'
>
> I was perched on the railway bridge that spanned

Coopers River. The water was usually low in the summer but that year it swirled furiously, cleaning the dustbowl of any flotsam as it went.

'Shut up, Bronnie, or I'll kick you in the box.'

'Like you'd dare. Like I'd let you live if you did. I bet you haven't even got pubes yet.'

'I have, but you're not seeing them.'

'Thanks be to God for small mercies. As if I'd ever want to see your three smelly pubes.

Last one in is a dirty old faggot,

Who'll end up drowned like Gordon McTaggart.'

Bronnie Hislop was three years older than me, a solid country girl in a pink and green, floral halter-neck bikini. Her pubic hair was abundant; you could see some of it growing outside the edges of her bikini. I didn't think girls were supposed to let that show, but I never said anything because she could deck me if she felt like it and she didn't half have a mouth on her. She knew stuff about me that I'd just as soon she kept to herself.

The other girls of Bronnie's age had stopped jumping from the bridge. They wore blue eyeshadow, and lay on an escarpment of baked mud that functioned as a beach when the water wasn't too high. They watched boys taking daring dives from the top of the box-girders, only venturing in themselves when the heat was overbearing. Bronnie hung around with me because the other girls didn't like her anymore. You had to go down to the river with someone. No one jumped off the bridge alone. Life was all too much like a Bruce Springsteen song out our way.

Bronnie especially hated Dinah because of what happened with her dad, Ron. Her mum caught them in Dinah's car out back of the pub. What they did is still unclear.

'What were they doing?' I asked Bronnie.

'I'm not telling you, you're too young.'

'Too young, I'm bloody thirteen! Was it *oral sex*, were they *masturbating* each other or was it,' I gulped on the words, '. . . *anal sex*?'

'Oh, you are so off! That's for me to know, and you *not* to find out. I don't know why you hung around with her. She was a real slag.'

'Oh yeah, Bronnie, and you'd know. If you ask me, your dad's the scumbag. My mum says he'll have a try at anything in frills if your mum so much as turns her head.'

'Shut up about Dad, alright. At least we've got some money for new clothes.'

'You didn't get a white dress for the Debs Ball.'

'I did, I just didn't wear it – and neither should most of those sluts!'

Bronnie sneered at the eye-shadow girls basking on the river's edge 'Sla-a-a-ags!' she yelled and took a huge leap off the bridge, howling like a banshee all the way. I followed – not wanting to drown in the river like Gordon McTaggart had five years before I was born.

No, I wouldn't fancy being at the receiving end of Marie Hislop's ire, pondered Rose. *Nor her Bronnie's, for that matter*. Bronwyn had given her mother no end of trouble with all that lesbian business. Between Bronnie's carrying on and Ron's running around, it was a wonder poor Marie hadn't got herself into trouble with those pills the doctor had her on for years. At least Berni had taken his business to the city with him – for the most part. It was easier for him *and* her there. It seemed to Rose that wherever this homosexual business went, trouble followed.

The cake was gone now, and so were the caterers. There were still about fifteen people wandering around. Rose felt quite unusual – as if she could drift between memories like a boat on a stormy old sea. Berni's death had rekindled her past, set it up like a book, page after page. She dreaded his upcoming autobiography. She knew she'd have to read it, but it would frustrate her that Berni had the last word – again. She didn't know why some people had to spell everything out and make such a to-do about it all. Private business should be kept private.

Rose felt a stab of heartburn, her reflux acting up. She shouldn't have eaten pastry, it was always the same. 'I suppose the gays have their stories too,' she thought to herself as the burn subsided. She flicked through a folder of articles by, and about, Elliot Bernard. She wondered whether Berni had been vain enough to keep them himself or if Blaise did all the collecting. She stumbled across one piece that rather confused her: '... The acting Dean of English, Professor Stuart Hughes, maintained that the part of Guy Mates in *Gridiron*, © 1981, was rumoured to have been performed by Elliot Bernard. These rumours have not been substantiated. As to the allegations about the proliferation of this material within the university campus, there has only ever been one cited in evidence. *Gridiron* went out of production in 1982 and was only available for Beta class viewing in the United States, or so say its distributors in Fyshwick, ACT, and our busy little *Honi Soit* supersleuths.'

Alpha, beta, gamma, delta. They have all those classes in America. Rose had seen it in films. Sororities or fraternities they call them. Still, why would only one class be allowed to read it? Perhaps Beta was the second year and they hadn't thought it suitable for students younger than that. Certainly Rose agreed you'd be wanting to keep Berni's books away from the younger ones. Goodness, the ideas his stories could put in their heads. Still, the article didn't really make sense. Nothing about her son ever did.

She came upon another cutting. A journalist making accusations about Berni's involvement in a Filipino mentoring scheme and linking him to some ghastly drowning at a beach 'popular with nudists and homosexuals'. Rose kept reading, though she didn't know why. Everything about her son seemed sordid in the telling. Why he'd want to keep any of these press clippings she couldn't begin to fathom, much less why Blaise would put them out for all to read.

Suddenly Blaise was at her side, cheeks redder than before, eyes ablaze as his name suggested. He'd been such a handsome boy when he was younger, but Rose couldn't see it now. He was drunk.

'Oh, Rose, don't read that. I'm so ashamed to see it now. He deserved it at the time, though. You know, I never told Elliot it was me.'

'What, *you* drowned this Filipino boy?' Blaise peered at the offending page, he chuckled.

'God no. I didn't kill anybody. Though I just about could have murdered your son then.'

'Well, I'm glad you didn't do that.'

'I was angry at him, you see, for writing *Je Louse*. I sha . . . spoke to this journalist, who got it into his head that Elliot was involved in a nasty murder.'

'You said Berni did it?'

'No . . . I . . . just didn't say he *didn*'t do it.'

'Oh, Blaise!' Rose was horrified.

'Well, how would you feel if *you* were Pascal in that novel?'

'Was that who Pascal was supposed to be?'

'Of course, I thought you'd know that.'

'I didn't know much about his life . . . or yours, for that

matter. I didn't need to know all the details – I got the picture. I haven't read his autobiography yet, and there's going to be no disguising us in that, is there?'

'Not a single figleaf to hide behind. I've read it several times. I can cope. I suppose after *Je Louse* I didn't have an ounce of mystery or dignity left.'

'What about me?' ventured Rose gingerly.

'I don't know whether you'll love it or hate it. He was obviously much more fond of you than he was of his dad or his brother.' Blaise felt a little sick all of a sudden at these frank disclosures he seemed helpless but to make. It was the demon drink. It was always the drink that created wild illusions of intimacy and sentimentality. Rose drained her own glass. She looked tired, but she wasn't suffering any illusions.

'That doesn't surprise me. Neither of them understood each other. Berni was too hot-headed and his father too proud. The Lord sent Berni as a lesson for me. His father never took any lessons from him that I could see, neither did his brother. It was all or nothing with Berni. He always expected the world to see things his way.' She turned back to the article. So what happened about this Filipino murder?'

'Well, that's what's so funny. There was no murder. The drowning was an accident. Elliot had been out of the country for a year, so it could hardly have had anything to do with him. Look.'

Blaise flicked forward a page. There was a retraction by the same journalist. 'Elliot threatened to make a huge legal issue of it with the paper and when he proved there had never been any such murder at that particular beach they were forced to retract the whole story and settle out of court. The journalist responsible had done nothing to verify the story and just rode with it on the back of all the other unsavoury Elliot Bernard publicity at the time.' Blaise glanced heavenwards. 'Sorry, Elliot, I so nearly told you.'

Rose wondered if Blaise was looking in the right direction. She often feared she wouldn't be seeing her son in the afterlife. The Bible was quite clear about that as far as she was concerned. '*Man shall not lie with another man as with a woman.*' Berni always laughed when she quoted things at him from the Bible. 'God, Mum, you wouldn't use a cookbook or an encyclopedia that was thousands of years old – so why the Bible? A man *can't* lie with a man as a woman. Think about it, mother, it's physically impossible.'

'You think you're too clever for the Lord? You'll be sorry, my boy – mark my words. "*Judgement is mine, saith the Lord*".'

'Exactly, Mum. So why do you have to take it upon yourself, huh? I get on just fine with Jesus and the gang and they're cool about me, so don't sweat, Mama.'

'Oh yes, go on and be glib. It's only because through

all of ... *this*, I still find love in my heart for you that I don't want to think of my son spending eternity *down there*.'

Berni would sigh heavily. He tired easily of these discussions. 'Mum, God made everything, didn't He?'

'Yes.'

'And He made everything with love.'

'Yes, and He saw that it was good.'

'He even made the Devil?'

'Well ... yes ... but the Devil turned against him. Got ideas.'

'Nevertheless, God made the Devil, so he must love him and be stronger than him?'

'Well, who's to say? A man can make a nuclear bomb and that's stronger than himself.'

'Yes, but only the once, in this finite mortal world. Alright, look at it this way: God is all-loving, all-forgiving, yes?'

'Well, yes, but He has his rules.'

'But He's all-powerful, isn't He?'

'He doesn't like punishing us, hurts Him more than us.'

'Pish posh, Mum! It hurts Him more than us to arbitrarily consign us to an eternity in the unimaginable horrors of hell? I don't think so. He's either all-forgiving or he's not. Having the power to forgive all, but deciding not to, could never be called all-forgiving. If he's all-powerful, all-loving and all-forgiving, he'd never send anyone to hell. My guess is that hell is the barren mental wilderness inhabited by all the fundamentalists who are so afraid of their own desires that they have to condemn everyone else who explores theirs. Even then, God is so kind he lets those people feel like they're on the right track or already in heaven because God loves us no matter what fools we are. If Jesus doesn't want me for a sunbeam, then I'll just have to go into service elsewhere.'

He went off on such tangents, did Berni. She didn't know what he was talking about half the time. Rose didn't think God would be impressed by Bernard Elliot's attempts to outsmart his Creator either, but who was she to say? She hoped Berni was right about the all-forgiving bit. It did strike her that if she could love Berni as she had, then God, being God, must have a good deal more love than herself. If that was the case, merciful God would be bound to send her son to heaven. Goodness knows she couldn't find it in her own heart or conscience to send him to hell, so how could the Lord?

'Rose?'

'Yes, Blaise.' She'd drifted off.

'What was the story with Dinah Carrisbush? It never gets resolved properly in the autobiography.'

'Oh, Dinah, now there's a tale. He had quite a crush on that Dinah. She was a nice enough lass but a bit on the tarty side, you know.'

'Oh, I don't think Berni would have been one to judge her for that?'

'No,' muttered Rose without a hint of irony. 'But plenty of others did. I meant to tell Berni before he ... left us. Perhaps it's not too late to put it in the book?'

'Perhaps not.'

'You see, it's very embarrassing for me. I tried to protect Berni.'

'From what?'

'Well Dinah got herself in ... in the family way.'

'No one gets *themselves* in the family way, Rose, even I know that!'

She cackled. 'Well, of course, and everyone thought it was Ron Hislop. After all, it wasn't just Marie who'd caught them out in Dinah's car. Others saw what went on too and people talk.'

Blaise giggled. 'Talk, in Nguurrambang, *never* ... So why were you protecting Berni?'

'Well ... I got it into my head that it might have been him, see? He was only thirteen or something but sometimes with boys, well, you just never know. And he was so sweet on her. I thought if he found out she was having a baby he might have got all carried away about it or something. It's really silly now I think back but if you'd known him then – oh, full of romantic notions, he was. To hear Berni go on about her back then! He thought Dinah should have been an actress or an air hostess, even a singer. But she was just an ordinary type really – attractive, but brighter lights had shone, if you know what I mean.' Rose laughed. 'I was too embarrassed to ask him, and I wouldn't have had the gall to confront Dinah about it. I know people are on about that sort of thing all the time these days, what with married teachers having babies to their thirteen-year-old students and everything, but we didn't talk about it so much thirty years ago.'

Blaise interrupted. 'But the baby wasn't Berni's anyway ... He never talked about Dinah *that* way in the book. He idolised her like a ... a ... movie star.'

'I know, I know. I was way off the track. But there was a bit more to it.

'Where are you now, Dinah? I never did find you again and you'd be in your sixties now.' People come and people go. Elliot scanned the page. He was doing well today, he'd found two typos. He wouldn't tell Sarah, though. She'd probably think he was on the mend.

> Sydney's first gift to its new arrivals is to render them blank slates. You can move there from any place else in the whole country and it's like you've got no past at all. You can make of yourself whatever you will. From a dirt-poor farmboy to landed gentry, from a high-school weakling to

a muscle Mary, and all it takes is the suspension of disbelief and a forked tongue. No one remembers you as an awkward adolescent, and if you're comely and well enough heeled, doors will open. You have no siblings to compete with, no parents who might embarrass you with their ordinariness or remind you of what's to come with their decrepitude and no tedious peers trying to lure you back into the Neolithic swamp.

You can't believe it when you first stand beside the Opera House and gaze across the harbour or when you look up at the block of apartments that was No. 96 on TV for all those years. Your brain nearly pops when you move into some squalid student house in Balmain and everyone is saying, 'Hey man, you wanna smoke some weed?' Well, of course, I did. It was 1978 and the decade demanded radicalism and contempt for authority. I started my vain search for Dinah. I scanned the phone book, rang all the other Carrisbushes and finally reached a number where a woman claimed to be her mother.

'Haven't seen her since she dropped around with the kiddie a couple of years back. Must have met some bloke and left town . . . Oh yeah, that's right, I got a card from her at Christmas, she went off up north with some of her people.'

'Her people?'

'Abos. She calls them "her people" these days. I tried to keep her away from them as a kid. Nothing but trouble, I told her. I taught her she was better than them, but she started working in some gallery when she came back from the country. Reckoned she was into their art or something.'

'So you're not her real mother?'

'I brought her up, that was real enough. Who are you, anyway?'

'A friend from the country. She and I were friends in Nguurrambang a few years back.'

'So you're not the kiddie's father?'

'No. Is Dinah Aboriginal?'

Her mother laughed. 'She thinks she is. We gave her a home and a chance and all we get is a kick in the face. Reckons we should have told her about her birth mother. We gave her every advantage, and she looked just like the other little girls.'

'And she has a baby?'

'Yes, a sweet little thing, Ginibi. It's Aboriginal for swan or something.'

'If you speak to her, could you say Berni Elliot was looking for her? I'll give you my number so she can get in touch.'

I never heard from her again. She must have moved cities. I thought back on things she said when I was younger. She used to laugh at how Elsie would say, 'Ladies don't drink in the bar here.' She'd cackle into her drink as she told me stories on the front porch and say, 'No ladies and no bloody abos.' I never had a clue what she meant.

How quickly I forgot the tedious bickerings of small-town life. Instead I went to hear concerts, lectures and kept my eye out for a bar which served cocktails in hollowed-out fruits. I heard Germaine Greer talk, went to a Patrick White speech. A friend and I tried to peer into his window one night after we'd had too many beers. We broke a trellis and sent the neighbour's dogs into a frenzy of barking as we crashed through Centennial Park's foliage, just like the prowler he wrote of, and together we fell breathless onto the grass. We lay staring at the stars, panting in the summer night air.

As our heightened senses normalised, we became aware of movement in the night, a rustling in the shrubs. The ghostly figures of men moving through the trees. 'Shshsh!' I hissed at my [name withheld] friend. We giggled like school kids, we were high on dope. The men were doing such things to each other – scandalous things! Appalling, blissful things that I would spend the next twenty years dissecting with words and performing with vigour and relish myself. I wasn't shocked or frightened, merely *liberated*. As Derek Jarman said before me, 'They were celebrating the corner of the garden that the Lord forgot to mention.'

I discovered a new species of life that night. My friend and I viewed it with awe and respect from our grassy knoll. This was a species of man that couldn't be documented or infiltrated from the outside. Like vampirism, it offered total pleasure but demanded total immersion. There were no weddings or debutante balls, no identifiable lifestyle nor even any legitimacy to it. A simple fraternity of the night. I was going to hell in a hand-basket, according to all received knowledge. And while I regret it not, pleasure is a terrible trap. A good servant but a wicked master.

'Well, for a start,' said Rose, 'Dinah just appeared from nowhere one summer and rented that house from the McClures. They've knocked it down now and some nice units are going up, but they owned half the town back then. They'd been trying to let it for six months and had to drop their price – I mean it wasn't as if they needed the money. Always too many houses and not enough tenants in Nguurrambang. Anyway, Berni must have been nine or ten when she moved in and she stayed for about four years. People talked, of course, because no one ever moves into that town unless they have good reason, and there's usually more leavers than comers. Dinah arrived with that Holden of hers full of clothes, bamboo furniture, incense, records – you name it – and she set herself up. Sailed into Wilma Edmonds' dress shop and got herself a job. Wilma said her references were fine, and she'd been needing some help.'

'I don't know how it started, but someone said she had a fella in the city and she'd take herself off to Sydney for weekends every now and again. I only knew she'd gone because Berni wouldn't be riding over to her house on his bike those weekends. He'd skulk about, asking me questions I never had the answers to. She'd been telling him about fancy parties and whatnot which used to get him worked up. I'd tell him he shouldn't pester her, that she had her own interests and so forth, but I gave up in the end. Dinah told me she was happy to have him around to listen to records with . . . I couldn't see the harm in it.'

'So who was she seeing in Sydney?' Blaise was amazed at the extent to which the brandy had drawn Rose out.

'That's where we got suspicious. Well, not me so much, I kept myself to myself, but Marie Hislop. You see, her husband had been taking off on "farming business" those very same weekends, said he had to do stuff in Sydney as well. He was a supplier to some big mills, so no one thought anything of it until her eldest son, Colin, said something.'

Blaise was getting a little lost. His own mother told similar rambling tales, as if by virtue of association or genes you automatically inhabited the same universe and were familiar with all the players. The trick was to get them to the meat.

'Colin's not in the biography.'

'I don't suppose he would be, he was a good ten years older than Berni. You see, he was the mechanic at the local garage. Dinah always took the car in there for the slightest rattle, but apart from her drives to Sydney she hardly used it. She lived right in town. Anyway she had it in there two weeks in a row and Colin noticed she'd only done one hundred or so miles. Sydney was at least 500 miles return and that's without any running about . . .'

'And, from that, everyone surmised she and Ron were having an affair?'

'That was just one of the things. Elsie heard Dinah and Ron talking in the pub. She said Dinah was upset. She must have told Ron she was pregnant . . . who knows. Whatever the case, Elsie said something to Wilma, who was in Marie's ear before you could say Jack Robinson. I think Wilma wanted to get rid of her from the shop so she stirred the pot.'

Blaise smiled. '*A truth that's told with bad intent beats all the lies you can invent.*'

'Precisely, and I wouldn't have wanted to live in that house for the next couple of years. After the baby was born, Dinah was at Ron for money. He sent her some, but she pressured him into going to Sydney to sign the child's birth certificate as its father. You can just imagine what Marie thought of that idea! Well, Ron wanted to see the child and Dinah was all funny about it. Finally she let him visit the baby – and you'll never guess. Black as the ace of spades, it was. Ron came back pleased as punch and I have to say it put my mind at rest as far as Berni was concerned. No one ever saw her after that, except Wilma who called in when she was in Sydney. Wilma said she'd gone quite strange. Still insisted Ron was the father. Goodness knows what she'd been up to.'

'You had better read the book, I think, Rose. I'd like to meet this Dinah myself.' Blaise picked up a few dishes. He swayed on his feet for a moment. Rose thought she ought to go but remembered she was staying there the night. Perhaps she should have gone to a hotel, after all. She nodded off in her chair to murmurs of conversation. A child-like demi-nocturne, peppered by stray laughs and the cold breeze from the open balcony door.

Her son's wake and another chapter she'd opened and closed in the book of her life. A dreamscape of old cars, farm gates, chook-houses and church flowers engulfed her. The jonquils and daffs would be in full bloom when she arrived home, so long as a sneaky Jack Frost hadn't flattened them in her absence. She'd be wanting something else to add a bit more colour to the vase, because they'd be sending prayers for Berni in this week's service. The arrangement would be for her son, so she'd make it special. Perhaps she'd buy some gladdies or orchids or bird of paradise flowers. There wasn't much around the yard this time of year and the hyacinths would be too short for the vase. Lovely though, hyacinths – not so morbid as those trumpet lilies most of them seem to go for at memorial services.

'Mum, Mum!'

'She's not here, Elliot, it's Blaise.'

'How come it's dark?'

'Probably because you were asleep when the sun went down. You want a cuddle? A blow job? More morphine?' Elliot laughed. 'More? I've got it running thick in my veins, lovey.'

'Good job you have too. That should keep you entertained.'

'This is not recreational drug use, is it?'

'Elliot, drugs are what you make of them. You told me that when I was just a nipper and you gave me my first ecstasy. I thought you were so worldly and dangerous back then. Of course I soon found out it was true.'

'Did you hate that it was true?'

'What do you reckon?'

'You're still here, I suppose.'

'It did exhaust me. I bit off more than I could chew.'

'Woodrow was the one who bit off more than he could chew,' giggled Elliot.

'Let's not talk about that hey, let's just not. Are you reading your book again? Here, let me read it out to you.'

'How dare you presume I'm straight?' Just one of the

badges I used to wear in my initial struggle for social obscurity. Real political action? I left that mantle to other men and women with more strength of character and a greater vision for change. I was boner-lazy. I still had the dogs of religion barking at my heels; they kept a lot of people from entering the kingdom of pleasure we were all so determined to tell the world we'd found.

In the space of twenty-odd years, homosexuality went from a psychological disorder and a criminal offence to something, well something else. A litmus test for people's tolerance perhaps, or a tedious game of patience? I thought of Dinah, the impotence she must have felt, a white imposter who could never have revealed her Aboriginality lest people deny it to her or it spoiled her chances of working in dress shops and sipping long drinks in bars. She knew all about that conundrum before I'd even met her.

I've told Dinah's story because I'm sure she saw something different in me. She let me dress up in fancy outfits, talk about whatever I liked with no subtle veil of disapproval ever coming between us. We had a whole book of drawings – dress designs for a shop I said we would open one day. Dinah never looked at me strangely for getting overenthusiastic about things that boys weren't supposed to be interested in. Her plight, wherever it took her, was different to mine and Bronnie Hislop's. Simple plights made difficult by other people's attitudes. And they were never even exciting intellectual adversaries, just lazy-minded ordinary folk who never had call to think outside the square.

An autobiography should not be a cerebral gripe about the discretionary allocation of Zeitgeists, and far be it from me to speculate as to how that process works. Perhaps we're sucked back into the eternal tunnel and reborn as everything we hated last time. Perhaps we choose our next path or perhaps – please, God – we just get to rest a while in some timeless, blissful consciousness. Whatever the scenario, I can heave a sigh of relief because it's out of my hands and I don't have to do a thing about it. I don't have my mother's fears about religion, and even its dogma is pretty fucking lame when you think about it. You can almost sense the vicar winking as he lays it on with a trowel.

If, on the other hand, the Church's theological dogma is correct and God has created someone far more deductive, rational and intellectually fair-minded than Himself – me – then I shall join loved, but forsaken, Lucifer in his theme park of lurid horrors and make of it what I can. God knows, in my day you could have hours of fun with a rusty bike, a vacated wasps' nest and an old tractor wheel. How much worse could it be than that – I mean really?

'Yes, I thought that would put you to sleep. Goodnight, sweetheart.' Blaise closed the door quietly behind him, vanishing on nurse-like footsteps down the corridor.

Conversations pass over your head when you get older. Rose found that. You sometimes lacked the information or zeal to become involved. She saw the impatience on shop assistants' faces when her fumbling arthritic fingers searched clumsily for coins in her purse. She'd never had her son's capacity for making demands. He must have mastered that in New York, where people fast talk and compete with each other all the time. She couldn't imagine anything worse. When he was living over there, she worried all the time that he'd be mugged or worse. Crazed drug addicts and bug-eyed people who'd been turfed out of mental hospitals – you only had to turn on the TV. She'd read what he wrote about that meat-packing district. She always hoped they were imaginary places or that he only wrote about those sorts of things – never went himself – but she knew she was fooling herself. If there was some kind of mischief, you could guarantee that her first-born son would be up to his neck in it.

Rose had nearly choked when she read that section in *Corpus Delicti* where he went to some place called 'Hell'. There were naked men suspended by chains 'hanging torpid in crystal stupors. Meaty, living imitations of the sides of beef and pork bellies that had hung rotting in decades prior. "Can I tempt you with some rump sir or is it the tongue you've your eye on?"' It fair gave her the willies all that stuff.

'Mum, Mum!' She'd drifted back. To where? Berni was there, just a boy on that rusty old girl's bike with a sissy bar his father had welded on, so he wouldn't be teased as much by the other kids. The pedals went around by themselves – it was a death machine, that bike. He never had any skin on the back of his ankles, thanks to those whirling, carnivorous pedals. His father should have fixed it, she'd said so a dozen times.

'Mum, it's Kelly. She's down by the creek, she can't get up. I think a snake's bit her.'

'Come on then, let's jump in the car. We'll go get her.' But she was gone. 'Dogs do that, Berni. They go away to die.' Poor Berni, he'd wept and wept, he couldn't have been more than eight or so. He wouldn't touch his tea, just sat on the step sniffling – and lo and behold if the old girl didn't turn up at tucker-time, fit as a fiddle if you'll please. Rose chuckled to herself in her semi-doze.

She couldn't remember how old that dog had been when Dad had to take it down the back, never to return. Des figured she was over twenty, but that didn't seem right. She'd heard of cats living to over twenty, but not dogs, though there'd be sure to be something about it in the *Guinness Book of Records*. That was the only book she remembered Des ever reading, and six consecutive years of it were still in his room at home. She'd check about the dogs when she got back. She'd asked Berni about it in the hospital.

'Can you remember when we got Kelly? Your brother can't.'

'No, and Dad waited until after I'd left to shoot her.'

'Don't say it like that, love. Poor Kelly'd lost control of her functions. It was the best thing.'

'My *functions* aren't exactly shipshape either, Mum.'

'You're not in pain, are you, love?'

'No, I just feel sick. Have you heard this joke?'

'What?'

'How good is life?'

'I don't know. How good is life?'

'That depends on the liver.'

You could go on for chapters about AIDS, you really could, but I don't suppose it would do anyone any good. Now in the 21st century, even as I suffer its contraindications, it already seems like some bygone Gothic plague. A dud square on the board-game of the 20th century. *Go directly to the grave, do not pass go, do not collect two hundred dollars.* Now it's been sent scurrying by a billion-dollar pharmaceutical industry, which has allowed me the curious privilege of living after my fashion. Historic tales, however recent, of stoicism and torment only bore the young, and they are the ones I've tried for so long to appeal to. Poor Blaise probably thinks he's the fire I chose to come home to and curl up by after I'd finished gobbling down all the children of the villages –

Greenwich and Darlinghurst. Maybe he is.

Youth requires no context or justification. When your body can do whatever you want it to and your mind is free to dream of future possibilities, the last thing you want to hear is constructive advice or golden nostalgia from some old Dr Seuss Onceler. You're too busy getting into delicious and terrifying pickles and scrapes.

The trouble with lust, men, or me – I'm not exactly sure which – is that I never really bought the package that love and sex were essentially synonymous. People don't realise that while they are silently envying me what may have appeared to be a seemingly endless series of fictional and biographical erotic encounters, I was just as likely envying them their monogamous contentment (if I was convinced it wasn't a sham). That's not to say that if I had my time over again, I would wish things any other way. I always knew what I was and what I was meant to be. Neither the teachings of the Nguurrambang Presbyterian Sunday School nor the Plague brought down upon my brethren could convince me otherwise. I now see AIDS as an epidemic of fear and nothing more. There was never anything to fear but fear itself. I guarantee, if I could get back all the energy I'd wasted on AIDS-related fear in the last twenty years, I'm sure I could live another ten.

Perhaps I was lucky I got to America before AIDS did, or at least before the media turned it into Munch's *Scream* and a three-ringed circus. I was twenty-one and enjoying a confidence and popularity unprecedented in my life. The fact that I was a graduate got me a couple of introductions with academics but the most feted of my meetings over there took place on a beach in Santa Cruz, where I attended a biennial Shakespeare festival. Talk about high-art low-art! I'd only seen one of the scheduled six shows when I met a bunch of guys on the beach. They were smoking pot, they were most certainly gay, and they were making a movie. There's one of those myths about Santa Cruz. They say a lot of people go missing there – and hell, I did for a few days when I went to work at Fantasia Real Productions. Who wouldn't want to be in the movies?

'You miss people, Mum. It doesn't matter whether they were good or bad.'

Rose looked up at the hospital bed. It had been getting difficult to know where he was in his mind sometimes. Berni had so many thoughts in his head and now, near the end, they seemed to fire off in all directions. She didn't know what was coming next.

'What, love? Who's bad?'

'Well, all of us sometimes, except maybe you. Blaise thinks he's happy with me, or was happy with me before this, but I know he'd just got used to me, to us. That's what most people do. They get used to something and call it happiness – they can't imagine anything else.'

'Good job they do,' muttered Rose, as she rummaged

in her bag for some Quick Eze. 'It wouldn't do for everyone to up and leave their families and friends for every passing fancy.'

'By Jove, mother, I think you're having a go at me.'

'Well, for pity's sake. It might just be that Blaise loves you. It's not all your parties and holidays that count on God's register, it's the sickness and health. Even your lot can't get off the hook from that one, believe you me.' She lined a new coloured thread up with the needle.

'I love it when you're dire, Mum. It's the Scottish in you, I can tell.'

Berni said it didn't matter whether your situation was one of marital bliss or torment. After forty years, you miss it just the same. He used to be on about how flawed marriage was as an institution. 'It enslaves women and makes men lazy and selfish.' Still, people had been doing it since time immemorial – and now Berni's lot were entitled to it as well, so how bad could it be?

'Why would you make such a fuss if it wasn't worth the having, Berni?'

'I never asked for it, Mum, just legal recognition of partners. I'm happy to buy my own white goods and homewares. I never wanted a registry at David Jones.'

'It's not about things. It doubles the joy and halves the sorrow, that's what the Church says'.

'You ask Blaise if having to look after an invalid for this

past few months halves the sorrow. I bet he'd say it's doubled. Ask Blaise if putting up with Elliot Bernard's hissy fits and anonymous phone calls doubles the joy. He'd probably say yes, because he's sweet enough to, but at the end of the day my victories were mine and he got pushed to the side, forgotten in the stampede of attention I received with each new book.'

It was the drugs that made him rabbit on like that, she was sure. But she tried to indulge him none the less.

'But Berni, love, what difference does it make? What choice do you have but to make a life with someone? Not everyone wants for themselves the way you do. You're like your father in that regard, you know. I bet you never thought you'd hear anyone say that, but it's true. He wanted to have the best yields, the biggest farm – he was going to show Merv McClure and Ron Hislop. When you were only one year old, he bought that extra 200 acres of useless salt flat from Merv. I told him he shouldn't, but he had his heart set and Merv had the gift of the gab. More money from the bank, more back-breaking work. He never had the money to pay workers the way some of the others did. The truth is, if we'd sold half that farm off in 1968 when one of those fertiliser mobs came through with their generous offers and company farmers, we'd have been set for life. Twice the money for half the work.'

'You should've made him sell. It was your farm, too.'

'I said my piece. That's all you can do. I suppose Blaise should have made you stop drinking, then you might still have your health.'

'So you're saying Dad was stubborn, and I'm stubborn.'

She nodded. 'I fell for your father because I believed in him. I made my life and it wasn't such a bad one . . .'

'"Wasn't such a bad one." Less was always more for you, wasn't it, Mum?'

'What you don't know you don't miss.' She bit the thread off with her teeth.

'So I suppose you would rather we hadn't put your work in that craft exhibition?'

'That was a lovely surprise.'

'But you could have made a career for yourself if you'd wanted. You could have done classes for the Country Women's Association and spoken about craft to National Party conferences. Who knows how far you could have gone?'

'It's still me, me, me – isn't it, Berni? There's not enough room in the world for all of us to make a lot of racket. It's the humble folk who do the real work.'

'Yes, and it's the meek who'll inherit the earth.'

'Exactly.'

'You don't even see what an ironic and grim little prophecy that is, do you, Mum? Remember when it didn't rain for three years and the soil just slipped through your fingers like sand? I want to leave you and Blaise something more than that. My legacy might not even be something you like. But it is something.'

The glass door to the balcony blew wide open, a chilly breeze was coming in off the water. It was too cold to put up with now, so Rose went to close it. She looked down at the street below, the water beyond and lights twinkling on the North Shore. Your son dies and all those lights keep twinkling, all the people in the other flats keep laughing and their cooking smells fill your nose. She closed the door and went into the kitchen to make a cuppa. People were still drinking and talking, some of them down the hall, some in the bedrooms and a couple in the dining room. There were still half a dozen bottles of pills in the kitchen – mostly sleeping pills and sedatives. She tipped them into the rubbish. It would only upset Blaise to get rid of them later. In the fridge was a little bottle of liquid aroma which she thought would be a good thing to put in an aromatherapy burner to get rid of the cigarette smells. She found one on the shelf. Rose unscrewed the top of the bottle, sniffed it and nearly passed out. She decided the existing odours were preferable.

With a throbbing head, she went back to her spot on the sofa. 'Sickening stuff, who'd ever want a room to smell like that? Old socks and mildew.' She'd have liked to go to the guest bedroom, but thought she should wait until everyone had left. She picked up some school reports from Berni's shrine, grade five, 1971, all Bs and Cs. Form 2, 1974, a B+ for English, Bs and Cs for the rest and E for phys ed. Neither of the boys got As very often. She'd never thought there was much in it as far as brains went, but she could see now that Berni had gifts Des could never aspire to.

She picked up an article from her local paper. It was the interview he'd done when he came up to the schools on that Vitalteen road-show. 'You can't believe what your report tells you. Your aptitude is in your heart, not in the report card. The thing to remember is that neither teachers nor parents can interpret your dreams and desires for you. It might seem terrible in the country to be gay or lesbian – but in the city it's not so bad, it's even a happy thing to choose. If you were made gay, then you were meant to be that way – and if your friends and family hate you for a year or so, let them. It beats hating yourself for your whole life. There are help-lines and networks you can contact, so you won't have to do it on your own. Don't let the bullies of the playground rule the world. You know you're better than they are. You always knew that, didn't you?'

What Berni hadn't kept was the barrage of letters that followed in the ensuing weeks. 'Keep the homos away from our kids', 'Gays recruiting at a school near you', 'Elliot

Bernard trawls the dead for homo converts'. Rose agreed that the suicides among teenagers were a terrible thing, but to say it was because of being gay was just too much of a leap for her. They had no figures to prove it. 'Dead kids don't come out, Mum,' Berni had said. There were a few mothers who spoke at those schools; they had stories to break your heart. Even Marie, after all she'd been through with Bronwyn, sent Rose a card saying she thought what Berni had done might have been a help to some of *them*.

Pornography and nausea never mixed. Even reading about it could be too much. What the heck. Elliot made his bed and he would sleep in it. Or toss and turn sickeningly for another of those long nights of the soul.

> 'If you can't get the accent right, don't speak . . . I guess we can dub dialogue but no one is going to believe an Oorrstralian would be in a gridiron team.'
>
> The 'on the field footage' had real players, not us. Hulking great hetero all-American jocks seen from afar and filmed surreptitiously. They had no idea that their real-life scrums were an overture to us preening high-school nancy-boys, all frocked-up in football gear. We were there for the locker-room scene only. We had mud all over us – a make-up girl had done all that. We just had to shower off the mud – and that's when the fun began.

'Cool tackle, bro'.' Then I was supposed to grab my 'tackle' and say, 'You want a piece of this, man?'

You can imagine where it went from there. We had blacks on the team, Hispanics, Italians and a Tommy Hilfiger couple who looked Ivy League, just as long as they kept their mouths closed. We used the changing room of a gym the producer owned. It all had to be filmed after ten p.m. when the joint had closed. It struck me as highly unlikely that true blue hetero jocks would have G-string tan-lines when they stripped off. Similarly, I wouldn't have expected them to wear those arseless undies with the elastic ab panels, but hey, who am I to say? I wasn't the art director – we don't got none of them on our set.

Making *Gridiron* was potentially one of the most stupid and short-sighted things I did in my creative career, but I don't regret it – and at least my mother never saw it (or knew about it). Pornography is an ambition to punish the parent, someone once wrote. I never had that sort of conscious malice. It would have been a more punishing move had I wanted to become a serious actor, the kiss of death. The first thing that always surfaces for Hollywood stars are those unfortunate photos and movies they did when they were really hungry. I thought $750 was good money for a couple of nights' work (clever porn stars, and I believe there is such a thing these days, get royalty contracts).

Pornography only becomes a skeleton in the closet if

one suddenly becomes born-again in later years or wants to embark on a respectable career, or a political one – which of course demands pristine appearances but far more corrupt manoeuvres than any I can be seen doing as the inimitable Guy Mates in *Gridiron*. I never thought it would come back to haunt me. I thought it would be lost, destroyed. I never thought I'd be someone who could be damaged by such things. Jump first, look later – that was me. Who would ever want to see those lurid colours, those mustachioed clones of the halcyon pre-AIDS eighties? My students, of course.

Pornography is to gay men what glossy fashion magazines are to heterosexual women, cornerstones to our neurosis. It makes us desire the impossible, slaver over the unobtainable and forever feel like we are undeserving of true beauty (and unworthy of large penises). Well, perhaps on my death, *Gridiron* will be re-released, like the movies of so many other porn-stars who vanished in shabby motels and trailer-parks to the wiles of the plague, narcotics and unfathomable acts of senseless violence and auto-eroticism.

Rose had tried to talk to Bob about their son from time to time over the years. It was best when he'd had a beer or two and was seated on the front porch, keeping tabs on passing cars and speculating about how well neighbours would be doing with their crops that particular year. Berni may have had books published and fancy launches, but only she had ever been to any of them. 'Can't have two away from the farm at once,' he'd say. It was rot, of course. There was nothing to stop them going to Sydney for a couple of days but Rose was just as happy to go on her own.

Bob would talk sparingly to the neighbours and business acquaintances about their eldest son: 'Berni, he teaches – lectures – in the city. University of Sydney, English. Writes a few books, but you'd have to ask Rose about those. She's the reader. We lost Des to some mob in WA. Money was too good to keep him on the farm with his old man.'

Rose knew that when it came to your nearest and dearest, it was sometimes harder to say important things. She would never have told her husband she was right about the extra land he'd bought. It was a waste of money and then it became a millstone. Men were difficult like that, they'd kid themselves about their victories, rather than have their pride wounded. Women learn young to work their way around that and, for all your Women's Lib and discrimination and what-have-you, nothing much changes on the farm.

Marie was better than her at throwing a temper tantrum – but, of course, she had plenty of threats she could wield, too. Bob had never been the womanising type. He never even used to go to the pub with the other fellas. Sometimes Rose had wished he had, it would have given her some space to herself.

'Go and have a beer with Ron and Merv,' she'd gently nudge. 'It'd do you good to get off the farm for a bit.'

'Nagh, love. They'll be doing rounds, I'd only want one or two. It's all money, Rose.'

But Rose was sure they could afford a couple of beers down the pub.

Berni, on the other hand, loved his wine. She'd never thought it a problem. She'd thought Des was the drinker. In the end, Berni couldn't even have a single glass without feeling sick. 'When you can't enjoy a glass of wine, Mum, you know the universe is trying to tell you something.' Wine was nothing compared to morphine, though. Shocking stuff that, it had him wafting away in all directions. He'd be talking normally and then he'd be off.

'Blaise is coming in any old tick, Berni, so I'll love you and leave you and come back tomorrow.'

'They might have been by then.'

'Who, love?'

'I don't know their names but they seemed quite nice. Blaise can't drive the car, it's left-handed. There's never anywhere to park in New York. He'll get into trouble.'

'He can drive, Berni, he dropped me off this morning. It's just a normal car, your Golf, the blue one.'

'But it's not fitted to Australian specifications or standards. It needs to be reconfigured. Everything must be reconfigured.'

He started to get distressed. Rose never knew what to say when he got like that. She panicked and felt herself drifting into unfathomable and terrifying depths. Cosmic winds sprang up from nowhere and dark places could be glimpsed in the depths of her son's eyes. With her husband there'd been so few words. He was a stoic, but Berni was like a compass in the Bermuda Triangle. She feared he'd never find his way home.

'Blaise'll be fine, you'll see.'

'I bet he's with that Woodrow. They had an Alfa Romeo but it got wrecked. Hail. There's more where that came from. Earthquakes. Tornadoes, too, if you don't get your bearings right.'

'That was years ago, Berni.'

'That's what you think. I'm not stupid, Mum. I'm not stupid. Woodrow would stop at nothing.'

She snapped out of her trance, which had begun to turn nasty.

'Rose, I'm going now.'

She looked up at Teresa, who still had sunglasses on top of her head even though it had grown dark outside long ago.

'Do you think you'll cope with these remaining loudmouths?'

'I dare say, love.'

'Don't forget about the needlework, I'll try and get back tomorrow before you head home. I'll run you to the station. Your train's at two, isn't it?'

'Yes, that's kind of you. Nice to see you again, Teresa.'

'Home,' thought Rose. What did she want with that big house now? She ought to move into one of the units in town. The nice ones on the corner of Ray Street and Fergus Avenue. They'd got central heating and even a nurse on call if you needed one. She sipped her tea and closed her eyes. A cold, sharp wind cut under the balcony door, whispering promises of unsettled rest and unpleasant dreams, but she gave in to it anyway. She was caught for a moment in a breezy hammock swinging between the conscious and unconscious. Caught between the Devil and the deep blue sea.

When Rose woke she had a blanket across her lap. Blaise must have put it over her. There was no one left in the lounge or the dining room, but she could hear voices and shouts coming from the bedroom. She needed to go to the toilet and she thought it best if she could safely occupy the spare room. It had been a big day and it was well after ten now. She'd dozed for an entire hour. She picked up her handbag as another round of cheers erupted from Berni and Blaise's room. It sounded like they were watching the football or something; the voices were loud and excited.

'There really was life before DVD?'

'Rewind, rewind, rewind. I want to see *that* again.'

'This VCR is a museum piece. Can you believe anyone even bought Beta players?'

'That bit, play it back. I want to see it once more.'

'Again! Poor Guy, you'll rupture him if he has to tackle them all over again.'

'You don't mind, do you, Matesie?' It was Blaise's voice.

'Now, in Australian rules, that would *definitely* be classed as holding the ball.'

They all shrieked with laughter.

'I think the tape's a bit stretched here.'

'The tape? I think Guy Mates is the one being stretched – to capacity.'

'Who's this dude? He looks like the Solo Man.'

'The what?'

'Never mind; you're too young to remember.'

'And what about him, the black guy?'

'Alas, Guy never gets to tackle him,' sighed Blaise.

Rose got to her feet carefully. The couch didn't give much support and she ached across the lower back. Her head thumped a little. She wasn't sure whether it was the drink or the aroma in the fridge that started it. It must be just a few close friends left now. Watching something on the telly.

'Oh, my God. He pulled out too late. What a mess – you never get that sort of shot these days.'

'Yes, it's a dangerous sport. No wonder mothers discourage their sons from rugby.'

'Wonder how many of these *players* are still even around?'

'Oh, don't.'

'Well, in a way, he's immortalised now, just as he wanted to be. Forever young and eternally active.'

'And caught in a loop. He would never have had the same partner this many times. Rewind.'

'Mindja tongue, queen,' shouted Blaise.

'No, just watch the rest, Jocks Downe is just about to *enter*. He's the coach, he reckons Guy Mates needs a dressing down after his appalling performance on the field.'

'So what happened to the other team – the Denver Broncos, or whatever they're called?'

'Well, they have different locker rooms – but don't worry, they'll have to share soon because their plumbing is about to go on the blink.'

'How do you know so much?'

'Oh, I had to house-sit here once. Blaise and Berni allowed me full access to their vids.'

'Not this one, you bastard. You must have turned our room upside down.'

'Breaches of privacy are the finest form of flattery. I like to know what's going on in my people's lives!'

Blaise grunted. 'Well, anyway. You *don't* get to see the Denver Broncos in this one. It's in *Gridiron II* – the sequel, which doesn't include our Mr Mates, sadly. Now watch this bit. This smile he does, it's a classic!'

Rose went to turn into the bathroom. She could quietly retire to the spare room now. No one was in there, but she thought she'd just let Blaise know she was off to bed. She popped her head around his bedroom door.

There were four of them, lying on the bed like teenagers watching the TV. She peered at the screen, expecting to see a football game, but it didn't look like that. No, they seemed to be in the change rooms. *Ooh, Lord, they'd no clothes on and* . . .

'Now this, watch this!' shouted Blaise.

Rose looked on in shock. It was pornography they were looking at. She'd never seen it before. Everyone was waiting for whatever Blaise was expecting – and then she saw it. The pink, sweating face of her son turned towards her, as another man rode his back. Berni's eyes looked heavy, like he was drunk or half-asleep, but he was smiling like the Devil.

'Ooh yeah, bug that tight ass, you mother-fucker!'

Rose felt glued to the spot when one of the boys noticed her. He smiled idiotically in her direction.

'Ahem, ahem.'

'What?'

'Turn it off,' he urged coarsely.

'Why?' Blaise was concentrating on his fast-forwarding. He wanted to get to the next Guy Mates scene. 'Here, this is it!'

'The *mother*,' growled the one who'd noticed Rose. It was 'the bitch' from the earlier conversation she'd heard.

'What?' He turned.

'Oh my God . . . Rose.'

Rose was lost. Truly gobsmacked for a moment, and most definitely lost for words.

'It's . . . it's . . . not what you think.'

She rocked to and fro but kept her footing. Something gave her an uncommon inner strength; she was more embarrassed than shocked, as the others stared at her with gaping mouths. Pink, children's cheeks that wanted slapping. Where was their guts, she thought, as anger of a type filtered its way through her fragile physique. Kiddies who'd just been caught playing doctors or 'a-bit-too-far', as Berni had called it when she'd caught him and that David Musgrove as youngsters.

'It's not what I think? It's not *Gridiron*, then? A guide to gridiron players of America.'

'I'm sorry, Rose. Yes. It is *Gridiron*, a pornographic movie Elliot made twenty-odd years ago.'

Rose stood for a moment. Blaise had paused the video player but the image wasn't perfectly still. It seemed to be trembling on the freeze frame, Berni's head shaking slightly from side to side. Berni's head that moments ago had been uttering those filthy words and sweating in its obscene congress now seemed to be saying 'NO, MUM.' The smile had a macabre, pathetic look to it. Rose, horrified though she was, wanted to see it. To see her son animated and alive – as alive as any human can ever be. But this screening wasn't for her, this was another society that would never invite her in. The blond fellow, the bitch, had said it himself, 'The mother.' *What else could she ever be but the goose who'd laid the golden egg?*

'I might not be a sophisticated woman, Blaise, but do you think for a minute that I didn't know Berni well enough to think him capable of this sort of thing? Lord, any sort of thing when it came to sex.' She felt tears of exhaustion filling her eyes – she didn't want them to show now. 'What Berni didn't realise ... What *none* of you realise is that you're not the only ones who ever had sex. You think a world that excludes women and children, and all the heartache that goes with raising a family is better? You imagine your sneaky ... smutty scheme of things to be some sort of superior, exclusive club. You think for every one of those sweating, grunting men on your video there's not a mother out there who raised him. A woman who raised a boy that was not so brave, strong and tough as the others. A boy who might very easily be crushed in the rough and tumble if he didn't have *her* there to see him through. You think it all comes down to a naughty time when Mum's not about. Well I'll tell you, Berni wouldn't have lasted a minute in Nguurrambang if he didn't have a mother like me. The Lord gave me my son so I'd know more of the world, whether I wanted to or not. And by Christ I do, so please don't lie to me, Blaise, when I ask you a question. It may have been too much for his dad, but I'll tell you this much: the life of Bernard Elliot was an easier one than that of his mother.'

Blaise turned the machine off and went to Rose, who still stood her ground in the doorway.

'I didn't mean to upset you. I didn't have the words to te ... I didn't have the courage to tell you that Elliot had been immortalised in more than just literature. He was always braver and more courageous than me.'

'And always more selfish too, I suspect.'

'He was selfish, I was lazy. Which is worse?'

'I don't know, Blaise. Laziness gets you into much less trouble.'

Blaise gulped. 'If you want ... if you'd like a copy of *Gridiron*, I can get one made for you.'

Rose thought for a moment, keeping the dumbstruck company of naughty children uneasily silent.

'I've some lovely pictures of Berni up home and I don't think that *Gridiron* ... Well, it's not really the way I knew him, is it? No, Blaise. I just came in to say I'm very tired and I might take myself off to bed in the spare room. I'll just leave you lot to your movies and see you in the morning, love.'

You can't lie to your mother, you can't lie with your mother and you can't lie about her. Mum always said I had to have the last word in everything. Mum, who always seemed to be cooking or knitting or pulling coloured cottons through fabric scraps. Mum, whose ripe red tomatoes were so delicious they could transport you to Sicily if you closed your eyes. Mum, who only went to one gallery opening, who wouldn't drive in the city. Rose Elliot, who wouldn't fly to America even if I paid. Marvellous Mum, who took off the cheap buttons on store-bought cardigans and replaced them with mother-of-pearl ones.

She'd never jump up and down, my mum. She'd never push herself forward and she's not one to spread malice, though she'll call a spade a spade. Well, Mum, you did say the meek would inherit the earth, but even the meek must set their aim a little higher than the scorched lands of home. And sometimes even a mother grows a strange crop that turns out to be of value to someone else. So here's to you, Mum, for letting strange fruit ripen in your own backyard, even if it was a little too tart for your jam recipes.